Phantom:
One Last Chance

First published in the UK in 2012 by Templar Publishing,

an imprint of The Templar Company Limited,

The Granary, North Street, Dorking, Surrey, RH4 1DN, UK

www.templarco.co.uk

Copyright © 2012 by Belinda Rapley

Cover design by Will Steele

Illustrations by Debbie Clark and Dave Shephard

Cover photo by Samantha Lamb

First edition

ISBN 978-1-84877-836-8

Printed and bound by CPI Group (UK) Ltd, Croydon, CR0 4YY

THE PONY DETECTIVES

Book Four

Phantom:
One Last Chance

by Belinda Rapley

templar

For Bun, my never-ending inspiration

Puffin & Rumpole,
our black and white rescue moggies

and Jerezano, my dapple grey Phantom

Rosie and Dancer

Mia and Wish

Alice and Scout

Charlie and Pirate

Chapter One

"I'VE found *more* black hairs in Wish's body brush," Mia said, her breath white in the frosty air of the tack room. She pointedly plucked them out and dropped the pink brush back into her grooming kit.

"That's hardly surprising", Rosie said, rubbing her gloved hands and blowing into them to warm them up, "when you think how many people have come to the farm to try out Pirate. Some of them must have accidentally used your brushes to groom him instead of Charlie's."

Charlie had been rapidly outgrowing Pirate, her mischievous little bay pony, since the end of the summer and, after one final success in the showjumping ring at the beginning of October, she'd finally stopped riding him. Her parents had let her have a new horse on full loan but they couldn't afford to keep two ponies. So Charlie had reluctantly agreed to find a new rider for Pirate.

"Has everyone ridden him now?" Alice asked Charlie.

Charlie nodded, poking her dark brown elfin-cut hair back under her woolly hat. Mia, Rosie and Alice were Charlie's best friends and she trusted their opinion completely. So, the four of them had spent yesterday meeting people, interviewing them and seeing them ride. Charlie had wanted the evening to think about which rider would be best for Pirate, but as she sat in the tack room the next morning, she still wasn't convinced that any of them were right.

"So, all you've got to do now is make a decision," Mia said, opening her notebook. "Who, from this list, do you think most suits Pirate? Who would you want to take him on loan?"

"I don't know." Charlie sighed, reading and

re-reading the neatly written list that Mia was holding out to her. "How about none of them?"

Charlie had wanted to find someone local, so that Pirate wouldn't be moved far. The girls had helped her, writing out adverts and putting them up in the post office and at school. Lots of people had come to try him, but he was quick and tricky to ride and most had been frightened off, or Charlie had put them off on purpose, knowing they weren't right. But with Christmas two weeks away, her parents were starting to pile on the pressure for her to find someone who'd take on not just the riding, but the costs of his stabling, bedding, feed and shoeing too. And not only that, Charlie was finding it difficult fitting in the time to look after two ponies before and after school, alongside all her homework. None of it was making the decision any easier. Charlie scratched her head. "This really is impossible," she muttered grumpily.

"Look, we *can* work this out," Mia said,

sounding determined as she scanned down the list of names in her notebook, "after all, we've solved bigger problems than this before."

The girls grinned at each other and even Charlie forgot her worries for a second. At the beginning of the summer, the four of them had decided to call themselves The Pony Detectives, after they solved the mystery of a stolen showjumping pony called Moonlight. Since then, they'd had three more cases to investigate, but they desperately wanted a new one to get stuck into, however small.

"Mia's right," Alice agreed. "And seeing as mysteries are a bit thin on the ground at the moment, this is what we should be putting all our efforts into – finding Pirate's perfect partner."

"And with our track record," Rosie said, "once the Pony Detectives get on the case, Pirate will be sorted out in no time."

Charlie looked less convinced.

"Actually, it might be sorted out already,"

Mia said, tapping her notebook. "Look – there's only one person who's really keen *and* an okay rider: Megan Green."

The others groaned. Megan lived in the cottage across the field from Blackberry Farm and she desperately wanted to take Pirate on full loan.

"I'm sure she waits at her bedroom window, watching the yard for when we come back from a ride," Rosie said, "because she seems to know *exactly* when to come over."

"Normally just as we're about to sit down with a hot chocolate," Alice grinned.

Since Megan had first ridden Pirate a few days ago, after seeing the ad in the post office, she'd been popping over every five seconds to show Charlie a new exercise for Pirate that she'd thought of, or a new feed supplement she wanted to try to make his coat shine. She used any excuse to come to the yard so she could groom Pirate or trim his feathery legs, trying to prove to Charlie that she was his ideal partner.

"To be fair," Mia said, tossing her long, silky black hair over her shoulder as she put down the notebook and started flicking through the bumper Christmas issue of *Pony Mad*, "she is a pretty good rider."

"I know, but it's not her riding ability that's the problem," Charlie grumbled. "More her ridiculous plans to turn Pirate, the hairiest showjumper around, into a super-smart dressage pony. She hates jumping, which he loves, and Pirate *hates* flatwork, which is all she wants to do. It took everything just to persuade Megan to join us later this afternoon for a hack as part of the trial. She'd be happy just schooling him all the time. He'd die of boredom!"

"Well, if it's a dressage pony Megan wants," Mia said, flicking through *Pony Mad* to the ads at the back and circling one with a pink highlighter, "there's one in here for loan at Rockland Riding School, which isn't far away – 13.3 hands high, fourteen years old, experienced competition pony. Sounds ideal."

Suddenly, from outside, they heard a loud bleat, a cry and the clang of a metal gate being slammed shut.

"Well, here's your chance to tell her," Alice said as Mia put the magazine down. The next second the tack room door opened, letting in a blast of icy cold air. A small girl rushed in, her blonde pony tail bobbing from side to side. She was dressed head to toe in the neatest, most correct riding gear, holding a shiny red folder, and looking apologetic.

"Sorry, Hettie got past me again." Megan smiled as a black-faced sheep trotted past the tack room door, making a beeline for the feed room.

"I've told you a million times – *if* you insist on coming through the sheep field, *don't* open the gate," Rosie said, clambering to her feet. "Hettie's always lurking about, waiting for an opportunity to barge her way onto the yard so she can rummage around in the feed room."

"Why don't you just climb over the gate?" Alice asked, getting up with Rosie to help her catch Hettie and return the sheep to her field.

"I keep forgetting," Megan said lightly, holding up her folder. "I was too busy looking through this. I've found some really good schooling exercises I can't wait to try on Pirate and I've put them all onto a chart – look!"

Megan opened her folder and unclipped the ring binders. She carefully laid out three A4 pieces of paper which she'd sellotaped together to reveal an intricate plan of her exercise regime for Pirate. Big red, green and yellow arrows interweaved until they reached the final box which had gold stars all around it.

"All this work will take us to our first dressage test!" Megan breathed excitedly, pointing to the box. "I just wanted to prove to you how serious I am about taking on Pirate, Charlie. I thought this might help you make up your mind about letting me have him on loan – you said you'd let me know today, after our first hack. I know loads of people have tried him, but I watched everyone riding him from my window and I didn't think any of them got on with him like I did. Anyway, I'll just pin this up here..."

Beanie, Rosie's Jack Russell dog, eyed Megan suspiciously as she leaned over him to a spare bit of wall opposite the saddle racks. She never quite seemed to see poor Beanie and was always treading on him, squashing him or edging him off seats. She took some Blu-Tack from her pocket, then stuck the huge poster up, kneeling on the blanket box in front of her and nudging Beanie off of it in the process. As Alice and Rosie walked back into the tack room, Beanie shuffled crossly into the corner. Charlie looked at the chart, her face dropping as she realised how unimpressed Pirate would be by all the schooling Megan had planned for him, especially as there wasn't a single mention of hacking or jumping.

"Listen, Megan," Charlie began, "dressage

really isn't Pirate's thing. I mean, he's only got three speeds – jog, jog faster and flat out. That doesn't generally go down well with dressage judges, and you'll probably get fed up with him after a bit."

Megan shook her head vigorously and was about to interrupt, but Charlie continued.

"Look, there's a dressage pony being advertised in the latest *Pony Mad* – maybe that one would be better suited to all this?"

Charlie grabbed Mia's copy of *Pony Mad* and pointed to the highlighted ad. Megan glanced across, then shook her head again. "Don't worry, Charlie, I wouldn't get fed up with Pirate," she said, sounding determined. "And if you *do* let me take him on loan, I won't let you down, I promise!"

With that, Megan picked up Pirate's tack and stepped out onto the yard. Charlie sighed. Convincing Megan that Pirate wasn't her perfect pony was going to be harder than she'd thought.

Chapter Two

CHARLIE watched Pirate's ears prick as Megan placed his tack on the stable door. The little bay pony always got excited about being ridden, unlike Charlie's new horse, the fractious, delicate black thoroughbred, Phantom. His owner, Pixie, hadn't been experienced enough to handle him and had totally lost her confidence. She'd been excited about Charlie taking him on loan, especially after she found herself a new, straightforward and safe pony to part-share earlier in the autumn.

Charlie slid back the bolt and stepped cautiously into Phantom's stable. He was standing in the shadows, still and wary, his head up, ears slightly back. He was unresponsive and distant, almost like he was frozen, until Charlie stepped forward to take hold of his leather headcollar. Then he flinched and flattened his ears.

Phantom shook his head irritably as Charlie pulled back the thick stable rug from his back and quickly flicked her body brush over his thin silken coat. He danced about the stable, threatening to kick as Charlie placed the saddle on his light-framed back, tightening his girth as gently as possible. As Charlie untied him and tried to get the bit into his mouth, Phantom backed up into the corner of the stable, raising his head.

"Come on, Phantom," she whispered in frustration. It wasn't until she spoke that she realised that she'd been holding her breath and had been working in silence. Phantom finally opened his mouth, and she slipped the bit in. Then she hastily slid the top of the bridle over his ears and pulled out his neat forelock. Charlie breathed out, feeling exhausted after her daily battle just to get the black horse tacked up.

She'd had him for nearly three months now. At the start she'd had a few successes with him in showjumping competitions, but she was starting to wonder if that had been a fluke, because instead of getting any easier to handle and ride, he'd got worse. Much, much worse. At first she thought his cold, unaffectionate behaviour was down to being in a new yard with a new routine, and she'd been convinced that he'd warm to her and start to be friendly. But it felt like the black horse was more unreachable now than ever, as if he'd shrunk further and further inside himself, miles away from the outside world.

Charlie had tried everything. He was stabled next to his old friend, Wish, but he barely seemed to notice she was there. Charlie had given up turning him out, too, because all he would do was pace by the gate until he was brought in again. He never came to the front of his stable when Charlie arrived at the yard, or when she called him or carried his feed over. She hated to admit it, but she was starting to wonder whether she'd ever grow to love Phantom, however talented he might be.

"Faraway Phantom," she sighed to herself, remembering his show name. "Whoever named you got that completely right."

The black horse wrinkled his nose as Charlie tightened his girth another couple of holes, before leading him out of the stable into the frosted yard. She put her foot in the stirrup. Phantom skittered sideways and Charlie hopped after him, eventually managing to swing herself up into the saddle. His head was high, fighting her grip on the reins as she tried to make him wait for Megan and Pirate. Megan finally led Pirate out and fussed around him, checking that all the straps on his bridle were neatly tucked into their keepers.

Alice mounted Scout and waited in the yard, resting both her hands on her grey Connemara pony's neck to warm up her already frozen fingers. Her toes were numb with cold too, and she couldn't wait to get going. Scout began to paw the ground, getting impatient. Rosie, who had been ready for a while, hugged Dancer as the mare drifted round the yard, head down, hoovering up any last wisps of hay she could find. Once Megan had mounted, Mia led them over to the gate on Wish, who was covered by a dark pink exercise rug that matched Mia's thick fleece-lined jacket perfectly.

Alice leaned down from the saddle and scraped the gate shut after they'd all trooped out of the yard. They headed down the frozen rutted path which ran between the white crystal-tipped grass in the turnout paddock to their right and the schooling paddock on the left. The frosted post-and-rail fencing sparkled in the bright, silvery sun and great white plumes puffed from their ponies' nostrils with each step. While the other Pony Detectives chatted excitedly about Christmas and what presents they were planning to buy for their ponies, Charlie tried her best to keep an eye on Pirate and Megan. She kept glancing back over her shoulder, but Phantom's raking stride was so huge that she was always too far ahead to watch them properly.

When Charlie was riding Pirate she could laze in the saddle and join in the fun, but she had learned to keep her wits about her when she was on Phantom. The black horse high-stepped and snorted as they headed into the woods, where the ground became soft and spongy. He suddenly shot sideways as a pheasant dived across the path, and nearly deposited Charlie in a bush. She tried to stay relaxed, but her breathing got faster and faster. Phantom began to jog beneath her, his neck tight and his head high.

Charlie wished that she'd been able to turn Phantom out in his field so he could get rid of some of his energy before they went riding. But he didn't like being turned out, and the ground in the schooling paddock was so rock-hard that she hadn't been able to lunge or school him. Now it was like sitting on a ticking bomb, with pent-up nervous energy just waiting to explode.

"Steady, Phantom," Charlie said, her chest tightening in fear – she'd ridden him enough times to know what was about to happen next. The black horse's trot got faster and more unbalanced. As Charlie jolted in the saddle, he broke into a canter. His stride was short and bouncy, like a tightly coiled spring, and was almost impossible for Charlie to sit to. She tensed as she tried to slow him, but he fought her stiff hands, lengthening his stride.

Charlie could just make out the others' shouts behind her as she held her breath, but their words were lost in the chill wind that whipped her face, forcing tears from the corners of her eyes. She clung on grimly as Phantom began to race along the bridleway, branches snatching at her jacket. They flew down the narrow, winding path and she felt the familiar sick sensation in her stomach, knowing that now she was totally out of control.

The path was too narrow for her to try to turn Phantom and slow him down. Charlie would just have to hope she could cling on until he pulled himself up, but as he dodged around a low bush she tipped forward perilously and lost a stirrup. Phantom flung his head up in the air and tripped over a knotted tree root, stumbling and scraping the woodland floor with his nose. Charlie, already unseated, was thrown from the saddle. She closed her eyes tight, disoriented as she tumbled down and crashed into the bushes with an explosion of icy spray.

She lay there for a second, winded and shaken, then gingerly stood up, feeling sore and stiff all down her left side as she untangled herself from the brambles. Phantom pulled himself up ahead of her, his head high and his nostrils flaring as he snorted. As she heard the thudding of hooves on the path behind her Charlie dabbed her stinging cheek with a gloved finger. She brought it away and saw blood just as Alice pulled up behind her and squeaked at the sight.

"That looks nasty!" she gasped, squinting at the jagged bramble scratch across Charlie's face. "Does it hurt?"

Charlie nodded, not trusting herself to speak. It had been threatening for ages, but it was the first time she'd actually fallen from Phantom and it had been every bit as painful as she'd imagined it would be. Her eyes welled up and she turned away, looking towards Phantom.

Mia and Wish appeared a second later, closely followed by Megan and Pirate. The little bay charged up bright-eyed as if he'd loved every second of the high-speed chase. Megan, on the other hand, was looking a bit sick.

"I didn't realise he could go quite that fast," she gulped, catching her breath.

"Are you okay, Charlie?" Mia asked, seeing Charlie's hands shake as she touched her cheek again.

At that second Rosie appeared, puffing, while

Dancer's eyes goggled out on stalks at having been asked to canter flat out around so many bends.

"Ooh, that looks painful." Rosie winced as she caught sight of the livid scratch on her friend's cheek.

"I'd better get Phantom," Charlie said, turning and walking shakily towards her black horse, who had stopped further up the path, his ears pricked, staring into the woods. As Charlie approached, a girl suddenly stepped out onto the path right in front of Phantom. Charlie was about to call out to her to be careful when the girl gently took his reins, looking up at him in wonder. The black horse lowered his head and breathed on her. She reached up and patted his neck as if he was the quietest horse in the world.

Chapter Three

THE girl had long, wavy black hair and huge blue eyes with dark shadows under them. She looked about the same age as the others, but her frame was small and her face so pale that it was almost translucent. She was wrapped in a huge, red padded jacket and was wearing faded jeans and green wellies. Charlie hobbled up the path towards them, feeling an unwelcome tinge of jealousy as she watched Phantom stand calmly on a loose rein in front of the girl, his head low and his eyes half closing, as if he was under some kind of magical spell. It wasn't until Charlie had walked right up to them that the girl finally broke her connection with the black horse. Phantom snorted and raised his head, taking an uneasy step back. Charlie noticed, as the girl passed her Phantom's reins, that her eyes were glistening.

"Thanks," Charlie said, taking the reins from her. "Are you okay?"

The girl nodded unconvincingly. Then she sighed and shook her head. "Well, no, not really," she replied in a soft Irish accent as the rest of the Pony Detectives joined them. "I used to live near here years ago, and I thought I could remember my way through the woods, but I don't recognise any of it at all. I was trying to find an old bridge, one that my mum used to take me to. Only I couldn't find the bridge and I ended up totally lost. It feels like I've been wandering about in these woods for ever."

"Oh, do you mean Whispering Bridge?" Alice asked. "That's the one where everyone goes to make wishes! In the summer, the bottom of the stream sparkles with pennies dropped in there."

"Yes, that's the one!" the girl replied, her face lighting up.

"You're way off track," Mia told her, twisting in her saddle and pointing further into the wood. "If you follow the brook just beyond the path you'll get there, but it takes ages on foot."

"There *is* a short cut," Alice added, "but it's a pretty scary ride – we never go that way – far too twisty and hilly, and the path's always pretty tangled up."

"And all the walkers avoid it during the winter anyway," Rosie said. "The water rises really high, and the rocks around the bank get all slimy and slippery. Seriously dodgy."

The girl was still staring into the woods where Mia had pointed, as if she'd drifted into a different world. Then she shivered and looked back at the others. "Well, I guess I'd better try to get back. Only, I'm still kind of lost," she said shyly. "I don't suppose you could tell me how to get back to the village from here, could you?"

"Of course," Mia smiled. "We'll take you right the way home."

"Oh no, you don't need to do that," the girl said quickly. "I don't want to put you out."

"You aren't," Rosie said.

"And it's really not out of our way," Alice added, to reassure her. She could sense how lost the girl was, and it had nothing to do with not knowing her way back to the village.

The girl smiled. "Ok then, thanks."

Charlie pulled the reins over Phantom's head and ran the stirrups up on his saddle.

"Aren't you getting back on?" Mia asked, frowning. Charlie never walked anywhere when she could ride.

"Oh, I thought it would be nicer for..." Charlie looked towards the girl.

"Neve," she said quietly.

"I thought it would be nicer for Neve if I walked with her," Charlie said, not looking Mia in the eye. Something powerful was stopping her getting back into the saddle; it felt as if a switch inside her had been flicked, and the thought of it made her freeze. For the first time ever, she was too scared to ride. She just didn't trust Phantom. She clung onto his reins tightly as he fought against her, scuttling backwards and threatening to rear. Neve glanced over at her.

"Try loosening your grip a bit," she suggested "That way you're not giving your horse anything to fight against."

Charlie realised Neve was right – her fingers were locked with cold and fear, and she was rigidly hanging onto the reins. She softened her grip and Phantom shook his head, relaxed and lowered his neck slightly. She looked sideways at Neve, secretly impressed but also kicking herself for looking like a complete novice with her own horse.

Neve walked with her head down, quietly. Charlie noticed that she kept looking over at Phantom, as if she couldn't take her eyes off him. But at the same time, it was like she was miles away. They walked on in silence until they came to a fork in the bridleway.

"I think I'll take Pirate back now, if that's okay, Charlie?" Megan asked, still looking a bit wobbly.

"No probs," Charlie replied. "I'll see you back at the yard, Megan."

"Are you sure you should be carrying on?" Alice asked, concerned.

Charlie nodded, not particularly feeling up to another enthusiastic dressage conversation with Megan, let alone having to tell her that she couldn't take Pirate on loan. Megan turned a reluctant Pirate away from the others and jogged him up the right-hand path.

"Blackberry Farm, where Rosie lives and where we keep our ponies, is just up there," Alice told Neve. Neve nodded. "You can always pop round if you come out to the woods again."

"Thanks," Neve replied quietly, "but I'm going back to Ireland straight after Christmas, so I won't be around for long."

"Well, that's another couple of weeks yet and school breaks up this Thursday, so if you change your mind," Rosie said, "the offer's there."

Neve smiled up at her fleetingly, before looking down again. Together they walked along the bridleway until it joined a lane, which curved around the outskirts of the village. They turned off onto a smaller lane which led to the duck pond and post office, then saw an elderly couple looking up anxiously from a garden gate. The girls recognised the man at once as Mr McCuthers, the local large-animal vet. He'd come to Blackberry Farm to look after Mr Honeycott's sheep in the past and had checked out Scout when Alice had first taken him on loan. Mr McCuthers recognised the girls too and nodded to them.

"Thanks for bringing me back," Neve said quickly. "There are my grandparents."

She walked to the gate without looking back. The girls thought they had better leave her to it, but just as they were about to ride on, Dancer took Rosie by surprise, diving suddenly towards an evergreen bush in front of the house. Rosie tugged on the reins, but Dancer stubbornly refused to move, and the Pony Detectives couldn't help but overhear the conversation that had started between Neve and her grandparents.

"You've been gone ages, and you forgot your phone," the old woman, who they guessed was Neve's nan, said. Her soft Irish accent was the same as Neve's, and her face was etched with worry.

"I got lost," Neve explained. "Then I heard hoof beats and luckily I bumped into those guys and they brought me home."

"Well, it's nice that you've made some friends," Mr McCuthers said, looking uneasily at his wife. "They might even go to the same school you're joining in the new year."

"I don't need new friends – I've got lots back in Ireland, at my old school," Neve said, her voice wobbling. "And I've told you already, I'm not staying here, I want to go home!" With that she turned and ran up the path into the cottage.

Neve's grandparents looked at each other and shook their heads.

"Thanks for bringing Neve home," Mr McCuthers said, forcing a smile as he and Mrs McCuthers said goodbye to the girls.

"No problem," Mia smiled. Dancer finally backed out of the hedge and the Pony Detectives turned along the lane to head out of the village. Charlie felt a weight upon her. She looked over her shoulder and saw Neve's pale face pressed up against the bedroom window, her haunted eyes fixed on Phantom.

"Aren't you going to ride now we've dropped Neve off?" Alice asked.

"My leg's a bit too stiff," Charlie said, not before catching the questioning look on Mia's face.

"It'd be easier to ride then, wouldn't it?" Rosie asked. She'd been watching Charlie hobble fast to keep up with the black horse, who she noticed was fretting again, now that they'd left the village.

They turned off the lane back into the woods. Charlie felt as if her arms were being pulled out of their sockets each time Phantom shied and spooked along the path, and her fingers ached as he jerked and snatched at the reins.

"Is there anything he's *not* scared of?" Rosie asked, leaning down to hug Dancer. She felt grateful that her pony was too lazy to flap about most things, unlike Phantom, who had just leaped across the path ahead of them, again.

Charlie didn't answer. As she struggled to hold Phantom, she knew that right now, out of the two of them, it wasn't the black horse who was the most scared.

Chapter Four

BY the time they'd walked the ponies back, the afternoon light was fading fast. The air was feeling icier, and the darkening sky was completely free of cloud. Pirate rushed to the front of his stable and whickered, his ears pricked as he watched the other ponies spill into the yard. Charlie's scratched cheek stung as she untacked and settled Phantom for the night in his warm rugs. She filled his haynet and cracked the thin layer of ice in his water bucket before heading to the tack room with the others. As they pushed the door open, they found Megan looking much brighter. She quickly shut the copy of *Pony Mad* she was reading.

She looked as if she was about to launch into

a speech, but Charlie stopped her before she had a chance to get going.

"Um, about loaning Pirate," Charlie started awkwardly, as she hobbled over and sat down heavily on a blanket box, wondering how to put what she had to say. In the end, she decided to come straight out with it. "I... think it's best if I find someone else, someone who wants to have fun with him and do lots of jumping – I mean, that's what Pirate loves. I'm going to put up some more adverts. Sorry Megan."

"Oh, right," Megan said quietly. "Are you sure?"

Charlie nodded. Her parents might not be pleased, but Pirate would thank her for it.

"Well, okay then," Megan said, looking at the floor then picking up her red folder. "I guess I better get going."

She stood up and they watched her walk across to Pirate's stable, pat his stocky neck, then disappear round the corner. Suddenly Rosie jumped up and called out.

"Oh, and don't forget to..."

At that moment there was another cry, a bleat and a scuffle, then Hettie trotted past, heading to the feed room.

"Climb the gate."

Rosie sighed as she and Alice got up again, well practised after a few days of shepherding duty. They rushed out into the dark winter evening, shivering as they turned on the yard light, which glowed pale yellow. At that moment they heard a couple of cars crunch slowly up the bumpy drive that led to the yard.

"That'll be your mum, Charlie," Mia said, jumping up, "and my dad. We'd better feed and say goodnight to the ponies."

They hastily mixed feeds, dropping carrots and apples into the buckets before taking them out to the ponies, who whickered deeply, their nostrils fluttering at the sight of their dinner. The only horse that stayed back was Phantom. He stood stock still, like a statue, the whites of his eyes showing, until Charlie let herself out of his stable. Next she opened Pirate's door and held his bucket for a second as he dived into it, then she put it down on the floor and gave him a long hug. Charlie wasn't looking forward to showing her mum her scratched face – her mum would go mad – but Charlie couldn't avoid it. She gave Pirate one final pat, then walked slowly towards the gate, where her mum was standing. Charlie kept her head down, trying not to limp too much. As she got nearer her mum gasped.

"What happened to your face?" she asked, looking worried. Charlie winced as her mum gently guided her towards the yard light so she could get a better look.

"I fell off Phantom," Charlie said with a sigh.

Charlie's mum took a deep breath, sounding angry. "Well, from what you've told me about that horse I'm amazed it hasn't happened before. But this is getting serious, Charlie. Look at you, limping as well – next time it could be a lot worse.

He can't be trusted, and you're NOT to ride him again, not under any circumstances, until I can speak to Pixie's mum and work out what we do next. And if he does anything bad between now and then, he goes. Phantom's got one last chance, okay?"

Mia, Alice and Rosie waited for Charlie to protest, but to their amazement she just sighed again, then nodded and climbed into the welcome warmth of her mum's car. Alice jumped in beside her to get a lift home, chattering away anxiously to fill the tense silence as they pulled slowly up the track, away from Blackberry Farm.

Charlie traced patterns in the beads of condensation on the side window. She couldn't stop thinking about how easily Neve had handled Phantom. Charlie couldn't help feeling useless compared to Neve. She had been fine bumbling along with a pony like Pirate, but who was she trying to kid? She'd got lucky the first few times she'd competed on Phantom, and she'd let it go to her head. But Neve proved today that the black horse *wasn't* difficult, just that Charlie wasn't good enough to cope with a horse like him. And it wasn't as if Phantom would care for a second if he was taken away from Charlie, either – he was so cold and distant that he would leave without a backward glance. As Alice's chatter faded and silence filled the car, the patterns on the window began to blur. Charlie felt herself getting cross at how unfair everything was. She wished it could all return to how it had been – before she outgrew Pirate and before she'd ever set eyes on Phantom.

Chapter
Five

AFTER a final week at school filled with carol-singing, the Christmas play, a non-uniform day and exchanging tons of Christmas cards, the Pony Detectives couldn't wait to get to the yard on Friday. They had another pile of cards to deliver to their out-of-school friends, including Fran, who owned Hope Farm, the animal rescue centre.

"Our first official Christmas ride!" Rosie had squealed as they mixed their ponies' feeds first thing on Friday morning.

"Or cycle," Charlie added with a small smile. She wished she could just tack up Pirate and take him instead, but she was way too tall for him now and she knew it wouldn't be fair. The others sighed, feeling bad for her.

"We can fix some reindeer antlers on the handlebars," Rosie said, "and pretend the bike's Pirate."

While they waited for the ponies' breakfasts to go down, Charlie took Phantom out for his daily pick at some grass, so that he didn't spend all his time cooped up in his box. The others set about turning the yard into a grotto, covering the stable doors with their cards, lots of tinsel, baubles and fairy lights.

They tacked up, with antlers on their bridles and tinsel on their reins. Rosie had pulled a Father Christmas hat over her jockey skull cap. They'd all wrapped up in as many warm layers as they could find against the icy cold sky. Charlie sat on her bike, which Rosie had insisted on smothering with baubles and jingle bells, as well as the reindeer antlers, and they all rode over to the gate. Charlie scraped it open just as Mrs Honeycott came scuttling out of the cottage, holding a huge ceramic bowl in one arm and waving a tea towel around, warbling at them to wait.

"What *is* she up to now?" Rosie said, shaking her head. She was so used to her mum's batty behaviour that nothing surprised her any more.

"All of you have to stir the Christmas cake mix and make a wish before you disappear off!" Mrs Honeycott puffed. "I'm baking it this afternoon, and I didn't want you to miss your opportunity."

"Dancer, pay close attention to this, it involves you," Rosie said, whirling the spoon stiffly with one hand and holding Dancer off with the other as the mare tried to dip her moustached muzzle into the bowl. "I wish you'd pay more attention to me and far less to passing snacks, including cake mix!"

"Rosie!" Mia groaned. "Wishes are supposed to be secret!"

"But the Pony Detectives *always* share their secrets, so what's the big deal?' Rosie said, looking quite pleased with her clever reply.

She passed the spoon, like a baton, to Alice, who giggled and wished that Scout would always be happy. Alice leaned over to give the sticky spoon to Mia.

"I wish that Wish Me Luck wins even more red rosettes than last year, if that's actually possible!" Mia said, after pausing for a second to decide whether or not to wish out loud. "Charlie?"

Charlie took the spoon, dipping it in the gooey mix, and sighed. She paused for a moment, looking over to her black horse's stable. "I wish that Phantom gives me a sign, even a teeny one, that he likes me just a little bit. Coming to the front of his stable to say hello when I get to the yard would be nice. Oh, and that he lets me get near him just once without looking seriously cross."

"Er, you're making a wish, Charlie," Rosie said, "not asking for a miracle."

"What about Pirate?" Alice asked, scratching Scout's withers as they waited.

"That one's easy," Charlie smiled. "I wish that the perfect rider appears out of nowhere, who loves having fun, just like he does."

"Two miracles!" Rosie cried. "This needs to be one seriously powerful Christmas cake!"

"Oh, and the person who finds the coin once it's been baked gets a whole extra wish on top!" Mrs Honeycott beamed. "And I'm making some mince pies too – I'll put some in a tin for you in the hay barn."

She took the mixing bowl and the spoon back inside the cottage as the girls gathered up their ponies' reins and set off between the turnout and schooling paddocks. Pirate, who was turned out on his own, lifted his head from the grass as he heard the ponies. He took off, galloping and bucking, then skidding to a halt at the gate, his hooves sliding across the crisp frosty grass. His huge mane stuck up in every direction. Charlie stopped her bike and found him a mint from her pocket.

He hoovered it up, and as he crunched it noisily, Charlie gave him a hug. Then she jumped back on her bike and cycled on, looking back over her shoulder as the other Pony Detectives headed towards the woods. Her heart ached when she saw Pirate's little face. His ears were pricked and his eyes bright as he stood right up against the fence, watching them disappear without him, and not understanding why.

U U U U

Mia led the group as they entered the woods. Charlie cycled at the back, weaving the bike along the path behind Dancer. She giggled as the unruly pony attempted to clamp her teeth around any bit of foliage that looked even slightly green, much to Rosie's frustration. It was as Dancer dived off the path and towards a bush for about the hundredth time that Charlie noticed a flash of something white on the ground, poking out from under some leaves that Dancer's hoof had disturbed. Charlie braked.

"Hang on," she called forward to the others. "I think I've found something!"

As the rest of the Pony Detectives pulled up their ponies and turned round to look, Charlie stepped off the bike and leaned it against a tree. She shuffled the damp, mulchy leaves to one side with her gloves and picked up a rectangle of pale, whiteish shiny paper. It looked weathered, and the corner had a big crease from Dancer's large hoof. Charlie turned it over.

"It's a photo," she said, puzzled.

"What of?" Alice asked, peering to get a look.

"A horse," Charlie replied quietly, staring at the picture. For a second she was transfixed. "That's so weird – it looks just like Phantom!"

"It does, too," Rosie said, leaning over and squinting at it. "How odd is that?"

They all crowded together to get a better look at the photo of a beautiful but thin, wild-looking black thoroughbred in a red headcollar. The horse was being held by a small woman, dressed in jeans and a T-shirt, her black hair tied back. The shade from a riding hat almost covered her face.

"Look, there's a date on the back. It looks like this was taken… six years ago," Charlie said, flipping the picture back over and showing the others.

"I wonder who it belongs to?" Alice asked. "I can't see any clues in the picture."

"Ooh, hang on," Mia said, leaning down from Wish to study the photo more closely. "Do you think that might be Hope Farm in the background? Look! You can just see the corner of the sign on their gate."

The others peered at the picture which, like the writing on the back, had faded slightly with time. The edges were bent and scuffed.

"It might be," Rosie said uncertainly.

"Well, we're riding there to drop off a card anyway, so we can ask," Mia suggested. "If that *is* Hope Farm in the background, Fran Hope, who runs the place, might recognise the horse. Then we might be able to find out who the owner of the photo is."

"And then we could return it," Charlie agreed, intrigued by the picture.

They looked at each other and smiled. "It's not much of a mystery," Alice said, knowing the others were thinking the same as her, "but the Pony Detectives haven't had anything to do for ages, and this could count as a mini mystery, couldn't it?"

"Yes!" Mia and Rosie chorused, getting excited.

They rushed round to drop off their other cards, deciding to leave Hope Farm till last.

The wintry-looking lane leading to the farm twisted gently downhill between tall, bare hedges, their branches crusted in white and laden with red frost-dusted berries. Dancer picked her way down very slowly, her hooves sliding on the icy ground every few strides – so much so that Rosie had to concentrate hard and keep her reins a bit shorter, rather than riding at the buckle end like she normally did. Rosie puffed as the lane evened out and gave Dancer a squeeze to urge her to catch up with the others, producing a long-necked, goggly-eyed, shuffling trot from her mare.

They soon turned off into a field, which had a strip of grass around the edge. Charlie smiled, thinking that if she were riding Pirate he'd be bunny-hopping, desperate to gallop. Her smile faded as she remembered the time she'd taken Phantom along there and he'd flown out of control, his hooves thundering as Charlie had fought to pull him up before the vast hedge at the end. She quietly patted the bike, pretending it was Pirate.

Dancer managed to trip on every lump and bump going, catching Rosie by surprise each time. Alice and Charlie couldn't hold in their giggles, which set Rosie off too, just as Dancer almost tipped onto her nose, sliding Rosie up her neck. Mia shook her head at her friend's clumsiness as Wish carefully placed her delicate hooves without stumbling once.

"There it is," Mia pointed out once Rosie had recovered herself. They had reached a five-bar gate in the high hedge that edged the field and could see out onto the lane. Opposite was the entrance to Hope Farm, with its ancient post-and-rail fencing dividing a patchwork of paddocks and barns. A rutted dirt track led from the lane up to a large square stable yard with a huge three-storey blue-and-white cottage to the side.

The ponies clattered across the lane and onto the track. Charlie felt a tingle of nerves as she took the photo from her pocket and gave it one last look before clanging the gate shut behind them.

Chapter Six

AS the Pony Detectives got to the top of the drive, Fran Hope, who had begun rescuing badly treated animals nearly twenty years earlier, appeared from one of the fields carrying a knot of baler twine. Her curly brown hair was pulled back into a scrappy ponytail and she was covered in wisps of hay. Fran knew the girls well from sponsored rides and competitions held at Hope Farm, and she beamed at them, calling out her hellos. She opened the wooden gate with its weatherworn, hand-painted sign saying 'Hope Farm' and ushered them into the yard. They were immediately surrounded by a seething mass of dogs, snuffling and wagging their tails wildly. The girls jumped off their ponies and Charlie parked her bike in the corner.

"Now, what can I do for you?" Fran asked, wiping her hands on her navy jods.

"First of all, we brought you and all the animals a Christmas card," Rosie said, passing the slightly bent envelope to Fran.

"That's very thoughtful," Fran replied, smiling brightly. "Thanks."

"But that isn't all. We found a photo in the woods near us just after we left the yard today," Mia explained as Charlie pulled the picture out of her jacket pocket again, "and we thought that it might have been of a horse from here – you can just make out the sign I think. There's a date on the back: it was taken six years ago. We wondered if you knew anything about the horse, or who the picture might belong to, so we could return it to the owner."

Fran took the photo and gave a little start. Her eyes grew moist as she continued to stare at it, until finally, she smiled sadly. "Well, this was taken here all right, but you'll struggle to return it to its rightful owner," she said cryptically. "I think we'd better find somewhere to put your ponies for a while, then we can go inside."

The girls exchanged puzzled glances. Alice, Rosie and Mia untacked their ponies and tied them up in the sheltered yard, giving them small piles of sweet-smelling hay. Fran rooted out three rugs which had just come back from the cleaners and were almost the right size to keep the ponies warm. The girls followed her inside the rambling blue and white cottage and into the large flagstoned kitchen.

"Take a seat, take a seat," Fran said, immediately sloshing some milk into a saucepan on the stove. Every surface was covered in horse magazines, headcollars with frayed stitching, unconnected bits of bridle, numnahs, stirrup irons, and an assortment of cats and kittens. The girls had never been inside the higgledy-piggledy cottage before, and they smiled at each other as they cleared some chairs so they could all sit at the solid, old wooden table. A large brown hen wandered in through the huge dog flap in the door, and clucked around, pecking at the floor before head-nodding her way back out again.

"It's odd that this photo should come to light now, I must say," Fran said, putting mugs of hot chocolate down in front of each of them. She took a noisy slurp from one herself and looked at the photo again. "You found it in the woods, you say?"

The girls nodded. "Why is it odd?" Mia asked.

"Why?" Fran repeated, sadly. "Because both the horse and the woman standing next to her in this picture died not so long ago."

The girls gasped.

"No way!" Rosie said, feeling goosebumps race up her neck.

"I'm afraid so," Fran said. "The woman was my good friend Caitlin McCuthers. She was the daughter of the vet, Mr McCuthers, who lives in the village. He's treated all our animals for many years, right up until Caitlin's death a few weeks ago. He was coming up for retirement at the end of the year anyway, but he decided to stop work a bit earlier than planned. Don't blame him, either – I'd have done the same."

The girls suddenly looked at each other at the mention of Mr McCuthers – that was Neve's grandfather! But Fran didn't notice their glances, and before they had a chance to ask any questions, she carried on. "But I'm rushing ahead – I'd better start at the beginning… Caitlin loved it here and spent every spare second helping out when she was a teenager. Then, when she was old enough, I gave her a full-time paid job and she moved into the annexe next to this house. She was a natural with the mistreated horses and ponies that came through these gates. She had such patience and understanding, it was amazing to see. It was like she knew what each horse was thinking – she could really tune into them. Then Caitlin found out she was going to have a baby.

She wanted to carry on living and working here, so I agreed. Never knew much about the father – he disappeared as soon as the baby was born. But Caitlin's little girl grew up here and was always bobbing about the place, just like her mum."

"Neve?" Mia mouthed to the other girls as Fran took a gulp of her hot chocolate, lost in the photo. They shrugged, uncertain, then Fran continued. "Let me leave that there for a moment while we move to the horse. The horse in the picture is a mare called Fable. She was a thoroughbred – trickiest horse Caitlin and I had ever seen. Caitlin discovered her in the spring six years ago, while she was riding through the lanes on a hack. The mare was about to be loaded into a trailer. The man with her was being very mean, using a long whip and shouting at her. I remember Caitlin telling me that the mare turned to look at her and let out the most heartbreaking neigh, so she rode over to find out what was happening. She spoke to the man, a breeder called Tim Leech, who said he was taking the mare to the knacker's yard because she was dangerous and useless. Caitlin agreed to buy her for peanuts and led her away there and then. She called me, and I came out to meet her with the horsebox."

The girls were silent, stunned by Fran's story.

"We got Fable back here, but she arrived ready to give up on life. She was skin and bone, listless, with no interest in anything. It was like she didn't know we were there, she was so far lost within herself. But there was something so... so hauntingly special about her. She'd *been* something, we could tell. Caitlin was determined to find out Fable's history – she wouldn't give up, said it could be the key to turning her around and making her live again."

A kitten scrabbled up onto Alice's lap as she listened, transfixed.

"So Caitlin drove back to Tim Leech's yard," Fran continued. "He hadn't really wanted to talk, but he *did* say that Fable had just bred a foal, only the little scrap had died at just four months old. Tim wouldn't say any more, and got quite rude about all the questions Caitlin was asking. He told her to leave, but Caitlin wouldn't give up. So she asked about Tim in the local village.

"A shopkeeper who also had horses filled Caitlin in on what Tim had said about Fable's past. She'd started out life on the racetrack, but had been injured and was sold to be retrained. She proved to be talented – could jump anything you faced her with, apparently – but she had a delicate temperament and you had to know how to handle her. She wouldn't perform for just anyone. None of her owners took the time to understand her, they wanted a jumping machine. But instead they got a fractious mare who learned to use her teeth and her hooves to keep everyone at bay. She quickly got a reputation for being dangerous and the scared little mare got passed from owner to owner."

Mia shook her head. "That's so horrible."

"I know," Fran sighed, wiping her nose with

a huge hankie. "And *that's* how she finally ended up with the shady breeder, Tim Leech. Apparently he'd bragged about buying a top-class mare for a rock-bottom price – he hadn't cared about her having a bad reputation, as long as she could breed valuable foals. But she was so tricky to handle by then that he could hardly get near her. He used broom handles and whips. Once the foal – a colt – was born, Fable was fiercely protective of him. Tim had mentioned to the shopkeeper that it was making the foal as mad as the mare. So Tim weaned him early and took him away from Fable. The next time Tim came into the village, the shopkeeper asked after the foal. Tim said that he'd died and that the mare was bad luck."

"Losing her first foal devastated Fable. What we brought back to Hope Farm that spring day six years ago was a shell of a horse and not much more. But Fable changed – that photo you found was taken after she'd been here a few months.

If we go next door, I'll dig out some more."

The girls followed Fran into the hallway, taking their drinks with them. They stepped over a threadbare mat and an ancient, sleepy one-eyed pointer dog called Jasper, whose tail thumped lazily as they walked past him, and into a room with box files scattered everywhere. Dusty photographs and rainbows of faded rosettes covered every inch of wall space, some of the photos as much as twenty years old, showing Fran when she first started Hope Farm with only two donkeys and a retired racehorse.

"Six years ago… let's see, should be over here," Fran muttered, clambering over to the corner of the room, where there was a desk stacked high with big boxes with dates scribbled on the front. "Ah, here it is on top – that's handy."

She pulled off the lid and started to shuffle through the big A4 exercise book inside. "We always log every horse in, with pictures of them when they first arrive and as full a history as we can gather. Then we update it as they progress. We should have Fable's passport in here, too."

Charlie shifted forward as Fran, sitting in the large wooden chair at the desk, opened the book. She licked her finger and thumbed through the pages. "Ah..." she said, flicking backwards and forwards a few times to separate a couple of pages. There were some gaps in the text where photos had once been stuck down. The Sellotape was still in position. "Of course – Caitlin must have taken them when... when she left. And the passport – she must have taken that too. Still, now, where was I?"

"You said that you brought Fable here in the spring," Charlie prompted. She wanted to hear more, but at the same time she knew that the mare in the photo hadn't made it, and she wasn't sure she wanted to know about that bit.

"That's right," Fran continued, staring down at the notes on the page in front of her. "Caitlin worked tirelessly to bring Fable round. Once she knew the mare's background, with the poor handling and the loss of the foal she was so protective over, Caitlin knew what her approach should be. She used every herbal remedy she could think of and spent hours with her. Then, finally, the mare started to show signs of improvement, signs of interest. She suddenly started to realise that Caitlin was there, that other ponies were around, that there was grass under her feet. But the more she came to life, the less trusting she became, as if all her old fears were reawakened. Caitlin didn't give up though.

"Then, finally, the mare turned a corner. I'll never forget the day Fable actually whickered to Caitlin as she walked to the field, early in September. Just quietly, uncertainly at first, but Caitlin couldn't stop smiling. Or crying! After that the mare seemed to get stronger. It was slow, but she improved every day. One morning, she even took an apple from Caitlin's daughter – everyone felt like celebrating! But the next day... well, it came as a horrible shock to us all...

Fable got colic. Badly – twisted gut. Caitlin's dad, Mr McCuthers the vet, came out but there was nothing he could do, nothing anyone could have done."

Fran sighed, wiping a tear from her cheek. She cleared her throat. "That was six years ago now. Fable wasn't here that long, but her last months were good ones. Losing Fable so soon broke Caitlin's heart though, I know it did. She moved back to Ireland with her little girl soon afterwards. She'd grown up there before her parents came to England. She set up a rescue centre like this one near Dublin with a couple of friends. They called it Fable's Rest. Took the mare's ashes and buried them over there under an apple tree."

Fran held the photo and took a deep breath. "And now Caitlin's dead, too. I can barely believe it. Killed in a car crash just weeks ago. I didn't go over for the funeral; I couldn't leave all the horses and ponies here. Still, I know Caitlin would've understood."

They sat silently for a moment, then Fran frowned.

"So why would this photo turn up, six years later, in the woods by Blackberry Farm?" she asked.

"We think we know," Mia said. "You mentioned Caitlin's daughter. I think she might be connected to all this."

"Neve?" Fran said, rummaging inside the box again. "Mr and Mrs McCuthers brought her over with them when they came back from the funeral. Why, do you know her?"

"Not really. We bumped into her the other day," Mia explained.

"No wonder she was so pale," Rosie said, remembering the lost look in her face.

"She must be devastated about losing her mum," Alice said quietly.

"And about losing this picture," Charlie said, suddenly realising how precious it must be to her. She carefully put it back in her pocket, all thoughts of jealousy over Neve's handling of

Phantom long forgotten. "We'd better get it back to her as soon as possible."

"There was a diary in here I was going to show you," Fran continued, looking puzzled. "At least, I thought it was in here, but I must have put it somewhere else. Caitlin wrote in it, all about the months she spent with Fable – detailing what she tried to settle her. She thought it might be useful for dealing with other tricky horses that came to Hope Farm. Typical Caitlin, she always wanted to help as many as she possibly could."

"Sounds like you could do with that diary for Phantom," Rosie joked, nudging Charlie.

"Really?" Fran said, looking round the piles of boxes surrounding them. "Difficult, is he?"

Charlie nodded.

"That's an understatement," Alice said.

"Well, it's here somewhere," Fran said. "I'll dig it out and drop it off so you can have a read through. If it helps a horse in need, that's exactly what Caitlin would've wanted."

The girls thanked Fran and they all made to leave. Mia looked at the book lying open on the desk and frowned. The Sellotape which had been used to stick down the missing photos was clear and shiny. She leaned forward, peeled a piece back and touched it, as Fran walked to the door. She nudged the others.

"What?" Alice whispered.

"That tape," Mia said under her breath, "it's still sticky."

"Is that important?" Alice asked, quietly.

"If those photos had been taken out of that book six years ago, the tape would have dried out and gone brown by now," Mia replied, as they stepped out onto the yard to get the ponies ready. The others nodded.

"Looks like they disappeared *much* more recently," Rosie said, hugging Dancer.

Chapter Seven

THE girls rode along the bridleway, taking the long route home via the village so that Charlie could drop off the photo at Neve's grandparents' house.

As they rode back through the woods, Alice slipped her feet out of the stirrups, circling her ankles and trying to wiggle her toes. Her feet had turned into ice blocks, and as she leaned down to try to feel one she noticed a flash of red in the distance.

"There!" She pointed. "Neve!"

They peered ahead and saw Neve stooped over, raking her feet through the fallen leaves not far from where they'd bumped into her before. Neve stopped and waved, walking towards them but constantly sweeping the ground with her eyes as she came. Under her red coat she was wearing a black hoodie, pulled up over her head, and had a black scarf wrapped around her neck. As she got nearer her face looked even paler than when they'd last seen her; her eyes had dark shadows under them and her lips looked blue. She said a shivery hello, frowning slightly when she noticed Charlie was on her bike. Without thinking, Neve put her hands either side of Dancer's neck, trying to warm herself up. Dancer curled her head to look at her, her eyes soft rather than goggly, for once.

"Is this what you were looking for?" Mia asked as Charlie carefully drew the photo from her pocket.

Neve's face lit up in an instant and happy tears sprung to her eyes.

"We found it today just off the path, a bit further up from here," Alice explained.

"Thank you so much! I thought I'd lost it!"

she breathed, colour briefly coming into her cheeks. Then she looked again at Charlie. "Is... is your horse okay?"

"Oh, Mum's banned me from riding Phantom at the moment," she explained, feeling herself go pink and wondering what Neve must think of her. "After my fall last weekend, Mum put him on his final warning."

"What happens after that?" Neve asked, the colour draining from her face again.

"Well, I've only got him on loan," Charlie explained, "so I guess he could go back to his owner, but she gave me the ride because she's terrified by him. So, who knows, he might end up being sold unless I can figure him out pretty quickly."

Neve looked at the photo for a moment, deep in thought.

"My... my mum used to take her rescue horse, Fable, with her everywhere – she walked her all the way to Whispering Bridge with me once.

She spent as much time with her as she could," Neve said, her voice shaking slightly. "Fable didn't like it at first, but eventually she got used to Mum and learned to trust her. It... it really helped."

Charlie nodded, remembering what Fran had said about how dedicated Caitlin had been to Fable. She felt a rush of guilt – because of the way Phantom behaved, she'd pretty much given up trying to get to know him. She'd spent less and less time with him, not more.

Neve shivered.

"Do you fancy coming back with us for a hot chocolate and mince pie?" Mia asked. "You look half frozen."

Neve shook her head.

"Thanks, but I better get back to Nan and Granddad's, otherwise they'll start panicking again," she said quietly.

"Sure?" Rosie checked.

"Sure." Neve half smiled. "Although maybe I will some other time – it might stop Nan and

Granddad going on about me helping out at Hope Farm to give me something to do."

"We've just been there!" Charlie smiled, then realised what she'd said, quickly adding, "Fran helped us work out who the photo belonged to."

Neve flushed for a second, then stiffened. The girls felt awkward, knowing that Neve had realised that they knew about her mum and Fable.

"I'd love to help somewhere like Hope Farm," Rosie said, trying to lighten things up.

"I'm not going back there," Neve said darkly. "I... I can't."

A tear suddenly rolled down Neve's cheek, which she quickly brushed away. "I just want to go back to Ireland – back to my friends and all the ponies at Fable's Rest. I miss everyone so much... I'm sure I could go back there and live with Mum's friends, but my grandparents won't let me. Either way, I'm never going back to Hope Farm."

Neve sniffed and looked at the photo once more. "Anyway, thanks again for finding this."

She carefully slipped it into her inside coat pocket and turned away.

The girls stared after her tiny, forlorn figure as she disappeared back into the woods, then they joined the bridleway that led towards the village. None of them knew what to say.

As they headed to Blackberry Farm in thoughtful silence Charlie kept her head down, pedalling at the back. She couldn't help going over and over Fran's words about Caitlin and Fable. It was too late for Fable, but it didn't have to be for Phantom. Feeling ashamed, she thought about how she was pretty much ready to give up on the black horse, just like Fable's owners had been.

"Are you okay, Charlie?" Alice asked, holding Scout back for a second. Charlie looked up and realised that Mia and Rosie were looking down at her too.

"Kind of," she said. "I, well, I was wondering if I should call Mrs Millar, the dealer who Pixie bought Phantom from."

"What, to ask her to take him back?" Rosie asked, astonished.

"No, to see if I can find out more about Phantom's past," Charlie explained, suddenly feeling a bit shy as she admitted out loud what the other Pony Detectives could already see – that she was struggling to cope with her new horse. "Maybe it'll help me understand him better if I know more about what he's been through, like Caitlin did with Fable?"

"Sounds like a good plan to me," Alice smiled. Charlie smiled back. She didn't want to wait a second longer, and pulled out her mobile, resting her bike against one leg. The phone rang at the other end, then went to voicemail.

"Hello, Mrs Millar. It's Charlie here, Phantom's rider. I was wondering if you knew much about Phantom's life before he came to your yard? Or if you knew his old owner, so that I could speak to her? It's... it's really important. Thanks." Charlie began to smile excitedly, finally feeling that there might be a glimmer of hope.

But as they approached the track which led out of the woods between the turnout and schooling paddocks, Charlie's heart sank again. She'd expected to see Pirate's head poking over the gate to welcome them back. Only he wasn't there. Instead, she saw him standing in the far corner, looking away from them.

"Sulking," Rosie announced knowingly. Charlie sighed and called out to him, suspecting that Rosie was right. While the others took their ponies into the yard, Pirate turned, his ears pricked, then trotted jauntily across the field to the gate. Charlie picked up the headcollar from the post, where she'd slung it earlier, and went to put it on. Then she noticed that the lead rope wasn't attached to the central ring as normal: it was clipped onto the side ring. Charlie frowned, trying to remember if she'd changed it that morning, but she was sure she hadn't. She moved the lead rope back into its usual place, then slipped the headcollar on Pirate. Charlie patted him and did a double take. His mane normally spiked up all over the place, and fell both sides of his neck. But now it was lying smoothly on just one side. He lifted his nose to nuzzle her.

"You've eaten some mints!" Charlie gasped, as she smelled the coolness on his breath. It was ages since she'd given him that mint before they'd all gone out riding – the smell wouldn't have lingered *that* long. She turned and quickly trotted Pirate back into the yard. She popped him in his box then ran straight over to the tack room, where the girls had just dumped their saddles and bridles. She got to the door, just in time to hear Mia tutting loudly while she stared at her grooming kit.

"*Another* long black hair! In my dandy brush this time!" she cried. "What's going on?"

"It's hardly a mystery, Mia," Rosie said. "Hairs do float about and there are ponies with black hair on this yard."

"Considering I cleaned all my brushes last

night and brought them in with me this morning, *free from black hairs*," Mia huffed, "I think it is a mystery."

Rosie and Alice exchanged a smile, but Charlie chipped in.

"I think Mia's right," she said.

"Are you being serious?" Rosie asked, half laughing.

"Totally," Charlie nodded. "Someone's been here while we've been out."

Chapter Eight

"IS the hair in place?" Mia asked the next morning before the Pony Detectives set out. Alice and Charlie nodded. They were going to test Mia and Charlie's theory that someone had been into the tack room and used Mia's grooming kit while they were out riding. So they'd set a trap and taped one of Scout's grey tail hairs, which was almost see-through, across the tack-room door.

"Okay," Rosie said sceptically. "So now we go out and pin up adverts for loaning Pirate in the post office and on various trees – *again*. And, when we get back, if the hair isn't broken but there *are* black hairs in Mia's grooming kit, we know it's just the air that's been moving the hairs about."

"Correct," Mia agreed, "but if the hair *is* broken,

we know Charlie and me are right – someone's been sneaking onto the yard."

Rosie looked unconvinced, but the others felt a tingle go up their spines as they mounted. Charlie got onto her bike again, having turned out Pirate on his own in the paddock. They rode out onto Duck Lane and stuck to a walk all round the lanes on their way to the village. Then they cut back across the bridleway and into the woods, and pinned up postcard-sized adverts on a few of the big trees where bridleways forked off, hoping that as many people as possible would see them. Charlie sighed.

"This is the third time we've done this," she said, pressing in the final pin.

"Hopefully it will be the last," Mia said, trying to sound optimistic.

Suddenly Wish, Dancer and Scout all raised their heads at exactly the same time and stared into the depths of the woods.

"What have they seen?" Alice said, peering

through the lightly hanging mist at the bare tree trunks ahead. The wood looked empty.

"Come on – time to head back," Rosie said, thinking of the hot chocolate and her mum's mince pies sitting in a tin in the hay barn. They turned their ponies away, taking the path back to Blackberry Farm.

"Charlie, do you mind if we have a bit of a trot?" Alice asked, looking down at Charlie on her bike a bit guiltily.

"No, course not," Charlie said, wishing for the umpteenth time that she was still on Pirate, or at least on a Phantom that she could control. "See you back there."

Charlie smiled as the others set off, with Scout powering away at the front, Wish behind him, neatly arching her caramel neck, and Dancer trundling along at the back. As the hoofbeats and the calls of the girls faded, everything fell silent. Charlie heard a twig snap, and then another, echoing through the trees. She turned round, peering into the wood, but it was difficult to pinpoint where the noise had come from. She froze, holding her breath. Everything was eerily still.

"Must have been a deer or something," she whispered to herself, instinctively reaching out her hand to pat her bike as if it were Pirate. Her heart started to pound. She turned back and pushed off. With one glance over her shoulder, she began to pedal furiously to catch up with the others.

˘ ˘ ˘ ˘

When Charlie reached the yard, it was pandemonium.

"The hair's broken!" Mia called out as Charlie squeakily braked by the gate.

"And Hettie's loose!" Alice added, trying to shepherd the runaway sheep with one hand and hang onto Scout's reins with the other as her pony ducked in the opposite direction. Rosie was trying to help Alice, but Dancer seemed to have decided that sheep were on her list of things to be scared of, her eyes goggling wildly as she planted herself near her stable and refused to budge another inch.

Rosie passed Dancer's reins to Alice, then helped Charlie to usher a reluctant Hettie out of the yard and back into her field.

"There are black mane hairs wrapped round my mane comb," Mia said, holding Wish's reins at the buckle end as she ducked into the tack room.

Charlie doubled back to the turnout paddock, unsure what she'd find. But after discovering Pirate's mane had been combed the day before, she suspected that the black hairs would be linked to her pony again. He was standing in the far corner, his head over the post-and-rail fencing and looking out into the woods.

"Pirate!" she called. At first her little bay didn't respond, then when she called again he slowly turned and looked towards her. She climbed the gate, starting to panic in case anything had happened to him. She jogged over the rutted ground until she reached him, her cheeks puffing great white breaths. Pirate whickered softly to her. She glanced over him: he looked exactly the same as usual – except for his mane. It had been neatened so that it was hanging much more smartly than was normal. And there, in a small pile by the side of the fence, was a bundle of black hair.

Charlie stepped up to the fencing and peered over, but there was nothing to see except the bushes and tree trunks beyond. She strained to listen, but everything was silent, except for a few birds tweeting and the occasional rustle and flap of a pigeon in the trees above. Then she noticed that the leaf-strewn area just the other side of the fencing was the only bit that didn't have white frost over it, and the leaves had been flattened as if someone had sat there, watching. She frowned, then with one last sweeping glance out into the woods she turned to head back to the gate.

"Come on, Pirate," she said quietly, clicking

her tongue. Pirate followed her across the field and she put him back into his box as the others emerged from the tack room.

"We're heading to the hay barn," Alice told her. "Rosie's just getting the hot chocolates."

Charlie nodded, and they climbed the ladder and huddled together in the loft. Charlie kept an eye on the yard through a small hole in the barn wall. When Rosie joined them and everyone had snuggled into blankets, Mia found her notebook and her pen. She flipped it open, turning to a fresh page. At the top, she wrote 'Pirate'.

"I know we all want a new mystery to solve," Rosie said, slurping her drink as Pumpkin, the huge ginger yard cat, leaped onto her lap and tried to snaffle some of the cream from the top, "but isn't this one just a totally obvious case?"

"The fact that everything's focusing around Pirate," Alice agreed, "and with him being groomed and smartened up, it definitely points to one culprit."

"That and the presence of Hettie on the yard," Rosie added. "It *has* to be Megan."

"Maybe," Mia said, making some notes.

"For a starter, she can see from her window when we've left the yard," Charlie said, "so she knows when it's safe for her to come over."

"And she was desperate to prove that she was the perfect partner for Pirate," Alice said. "She put so much effort into that plan. I think that she's carrying on with it to get Pirate looking like a dressage pony so that Charlie will change her mind."

"Or so that if Charlie can't find anyone else for Pirate," Rosie added, "she can step back in and still be kind of on track."

"Really? I'm not so sure," Mia said, looking up from her notebook. "Didn't any of you notice anything odd in the tack room when we got back from that hack with her last week?"

"What kind of thing?" Charlie asked, looking up.

"Well, Megan looked pretty shaken up by how fast Pirate flew when we took off after Phantom," Mia pointed out. "And when we got back, she'd already taken her plan down from the wall."

"So you think Megan had already made up her mind not to loan Pirate," Charlie said, frowning, "even before I said anything?"

"It's possible," Mia said. "I didn't think that much of it at the time, but now, with all this going on, it might be relevant."

"But if you don't think it's Megan, how do you explain what's going on with the black hairs and Hettie?" Rosie asked, unconvinced.

"That's just it," Mia sighed. "I can't."

"So what do we do now?" Alice asked, as Rosie finished her hot chocolate and reached for the tin of mince pies.

"I think we should start to keep a watch on the yard," Mia suggested. "That way we can keep an eye out for Megan, or whoever the visitor might be, and catch them red-handed if they sneak in."

Suddenly Rosie squealed.

"What?" Charlie asked.

"Our stash of mince pies!" Rosie gasped. "They've all gone!"

Chapter Nine

THE next morning the four girls turned out their ponies, except for Phantom, who hated going in the field. They'd planned to hide on the yard all day so they could keep a lookout, which meant no riding. They mucked out, refilled haynets, scrubbed water buckets and swept the yard. Mrs Millar had texted Charlie, saying that she had got her message, was doing a bit of digging for information, and then would call.

Charlie stayed a while in Phantom's box. "Things will get better, I promise," she whispered, to convince herself as much as to persuade the black horse. Phantom stood warily, unmoving, at the back of the box. He turned his deep liquid eye on her, the whites showing, and Charlie felt a tingle of nerves run through her. He made her feel so tiny, with just one look. He still scared her, no matter what she tried to tell herself. She let herself out of the stable, and headed into Rosie's cottage with the others for some hot buttered toast and hot chocolate.

"Oh, I almost forgot," Mrs Honeycott said vaguely as she put the plates on the table. "There was something in the post for Charlie this morning."

"For Charlie?" Rosie asked. Mrs Honeycott scratched her nose with the end of a thin paintbrush which she'd found behind her ear. She frowned, looking taxed, before nodding her head.

"Yes, definitely Charlie," she confirmed, picking up the pile of red and white envelopes, stuffed with Christmas cards. In among the pile was a brown rectangular envelope which had been folded over at the end and stuck down with tape. Charlie's name and 'Blackberry Farm' were written on the front in thick marker pen, nothing more. Mrs Honeycott put the envelope on the table, narrowly avoiding a splodge of strawberry jam.

"This can't have been posted," Mia said, examining it. "There's no stamp or address."

"It must have been delivered by hand," Alice agreed, getting excited.

Charlie lifted it up and turned it over. It felt curiously solid as she carefully unpeeled the sealed end and then tipped it up. With a thud, a slim red hardback book fell onto the table. The word 'Diary' was foiled on the front in faded gold, along with the year.

"This is from six years ago," Mia whispered as the others held their breath, already realising what that meant. Charlie checked, but there was nothing else in the envelope.

Charlie opened the book and saw, on the first page, the flowing, hand-written words: 'Fable's diary'. She carefully turned the page and saw the next inscription, which she read aloud:

"This diary is dedicated to the memory of Fable and her dear little foal."

"It's Caitlin's diary!" Alice said, looking at it in awe. "Fran must have found it!"

"I'm going to start reading it today," Charlie said. She couldn't wait to get going. "Right now, in fact, as we're staying here all day!"

"Ooh, we can all read it by the fire in the living room!" Rosie said, picturing them curled up on the sofas around the Christmas tree eating piping-hot mince pies straight from the oven.

"We can't exactly keep a lookout from there," Mia corrected her. "I think we should hide in the tack room and use this opportunity to do a marathon tack-cleaning session. That way the yard's never left unguarded."

Rosie sank down in her chair. The thought of soaping and polishing her bridle all day under Mia's watchful eye filled her with gloom. She wished now that they were going on a marathon ride instead, despite the arctic temperatures.

Charlie frowned as she saw her Mum's number flash up on her phone.

"Is everything okay?" she asked, then listened quietly before adding, "No, no I didn't."

Charlie ended the call, looking thoughtful.

"Who was that?" Mia asked.

"It was Mum," Charlie explained. "The woman in the post office just called her to ask if I'd taken down the advert for Pirate early."

"Why?" Rosie asked.

"Because", Charlie said quietly, "it's gone."

U U U U

Alice suggested that they should check the other adverts they'd put up. Mia stayed behind with Rosie to keep watch on the yard, while Alice jumped bareback onto Scout and jogged him into the woods, Charlie biking beside her. They got to the fork in the bridleway and caught their breath, staring up at the bare tree.

"The pin's still there," Alice said.

"But no advert," Charlie puffed.

"Maybe someone who wants to loan Pirate has taken it?" Alice suggested.

"Maybe, although Mum didn't mention anyone else calling about him," Charlie reasoned.

They checked the final tree and found the same – a pin but no advert. Then they headed back to the yard and found Mia and Rosie in the tack room. Mia added a line in her notebook when they updated her.

"Megan might have taken them down so no one else saw them," Rosie said.

"That fits," Mia agreed, "if it's definitely Megan, that is."

"I guess we might find out today," Charlie said.

Mia organised Alice and Rosie as they stripped down their bridles into pieces. They had a bucket of warm water on the floor between them, with sponges and saddle soap at the ready. Just as they began Charlie opened the first page of the diary, sitting cross-legged on the blanket box with Beanie on one side of her and Pumpkin on her lap. She started to read aloud:

I'm writing this sitting under the cherry tree in the black horse's paddock. Right now she is very weak and it's like she's not aware of me being here, but at the same time I can tell that she'd rather that I wasn't here at all. The paddock's huge, but she still seems to think it's too small for both of us. But if I stay here long enough, I'm hoping that might just change.

The description hit Charlie – it sounded just like Phantom. He never responded to her presence much any more, yet it still felt as if he hated and resented it. In an instant, she knew exactly what to do.

"As cosy as it is in here," Charlie said, gently moving Pumpkin and standing up, "I think I should be reading this with Phantom. Caitlin wrote this while she was near Fable, so the mare could get used to her. I'm going to try the same with Phantom."

Charlie walked quietly over to Phantom's stable. As usual, the black horse was standing in the shadows in his freshly laid, thick straw bed, his coat glistening. He shook his head as Charlie let herself in, and tried to swing away from her as she caught his headcollar. She clipped him to the lead rope, which she tied loosely to the baler twine attached to the metal ring at the front of the stable, near his haynet so that he could still pick at it if he wanted to. The black horse reluctantly stood near her, stretching his lead rope as far as it would go so that he could keep as much distance between them as possible.

At first Charlie was alert to every twitch Phantom made, her heart racing with each thud of his back hoof or irritable swish of his tail. But the more absorbed she became with the black horse in the diary, the less aware she grew of Phantom. She gasped as she raced through Caitlin's early struggle to keep the mare alive. She felt her eyes well up as she got to the part when Caitlin truly feared that she was going to lose Fable, and smiled in relief at the happiness that spilled out on the page from Caitlin's pen, when the mare finally began to take an interest in the world around her.

As Charlie read on through blurred eyes, Caitlin described Fable's introduction to Molly the Hope Farm sheep and how Molly's solid, quiet presence seemed to settle her. Fable still didn't trust Caitlin to get too near, but she and Molly quickly became inseparable. Caitlin then began to patch together the life that Fable had endured before she finally ended up at Hope Farm. She even traced her original breeder, who described her as a cheeky, feisty foal, and clearly promising. But that part of her character was quickly forgotten as she gained a reputation and got labelled as 'difficult' instead. She'd been shipped about from new yard to new yard, with expectations of her ability high, but was given no time to settle. Her nature was delicate, and Caitlin could track the change in her behaviour as it became increasingly unsettled and fractious. Each owner had sold her on, keen to get rid of the tricky-to-handle mare, until she'd ended up, broken, misunderstood and unloved, with Tim Leech – the nasty breeder who was going to take her to the knackers' yard. Tim said that Fable was defensive, ill-tempered and dangerous. But Caitlin could see beyond that to a fragile horse of whom too much had been asked, too quickly. Caitlin had found her just minutes before it was too late. Now it was down to Caitlin and Molly to mend Fable, whose heart had finally cracked on the day that her foal had been taken from her.

Charlie felt a lump in her throat, and a tear

trickled down her cheek. She heard a big sigh, fluttering through velvety nostrils.

She looked up. She realised that while she'd been reading, Phantom had stopped standing so rigidly, and was no longer filling the box with his unease. She sat quietly for a second, looking at him. He was so beautiful, but she'd stopped seeing it. All she'd seen when she looked at Phantom in the last couple of months was trouble and bad manners, just as all Fable's owners had done with her. She'd lost sight of the little foal he'd once been. She suddenly realised that she'd learned more about Fable, a horse she'd never meet, in one morning than she had about Phantom after three months. Her eyes widened for a second as a thought struck her. What if Phantom was more like Fable than she realised: what if he was apprehensive and fearful underneath his scary behaviour too, rather than mean and unfriendly?

Suddenly Phantom started, and Charlie looked up to see Rosie, bringing her a steaming mug of hot chocolate. At once Phantom was transformed back into his grouchy self, and as Charlie stretched her cramped legs, she realised how bored and lonely Phantom must be, standing on his own in his stable for most of the time – especially as she hardly spent any time with him either. She let herself out and walked back to the tack room with Rosie.

"I'm going to take Phantom to pick at some grass," she said. "Is that okay?"

"I'd better come with you, just in case you need a hand," Mia suggested, placing her gleaming bridle on its hook, feeling a bit restless after spending so long hidden in the tack room.

"Ooh, me too!" Alice quickly volunteered. After cleaning her bridle to Mia's high standards, her fingers were aching, and if she heard the same Christmas songs on the radio one more time she might go crazy. She stood up and passed the lunge line to Charlie. "I can open gates, that sort of thing."

Rosie looked down at the mass of leather pieces still in a pile on the rug box, waiting to be put back together. She started to wish she'd spent less time playing with Beanie and more time concentrating on her bridle. "I guess that means I'm the one stuck here keeping an eye on the yard, then."

"You've got Beanie and Pumpkin to keep you company," Alice smiled.

As the other three disappeared out of the tack room, Beanie scrabbled at Rosie's knee, asking her to throw his squeaky toy again.

Charlie felt her heart quicken and her fingers shake as she clipped the lunge line to Phantom's headcollar and led him out of his stable. Alice ran and opened the gate. Charlie remembered what Neve had said about not holding him too tight. She held the lunge line loosely, so that he didn't have anything to fight against as he was led to the paddock. As she turned in through the open gate of the schooling field she glanced over and noticed Pirate grazing with the other ponies in the corner. Suddenly a robin flitted out of the bush beside her and spooked Phantom, who danced at the end of the line. Charlie knew that, for now, the black horse needed her full concentration.

Alice and Mia climbed onto the post-and-rail fencing, huddling up together to keep warm. Mia wrapped her big, fluffy pink scarf around both of them, and Alice tucked her gloved hands into her pockets. They watched as Charlie let the lunge line out. At first Phantom stood, with his head up, then slowly he began to dip and nibble icy grass, raising his head and staring into the distance between bites, and starting at sounds only he could hear. But as Phantom started to relax, so too, Mia and Alice noticed as they glanced at each other with a smile, did Charlie.

They were starting to feel the numb chill of the afternoon through their thick layers, and their noses, fingers and toes were beginning to freeze.

Then they heard Beanie barking excitedly on the yard.

Phantom started at the sound and Charlie looked anxiously at him. She took a step nearer and reached out to pat him, but he lifted his head and shied sideways. She sighed, but reminded herself that Caitlin had only ever taken tiny steps forward and that she shouldn't race ahead and then get frustrated.

Charlie walked over to Mia and Alice, leading Phantom, who was warily keeping his distance. "I'm going to head back," she said to them.

"I bet Rosie's bridle's still in pieces when you get there," Mia said.

Suddenly they heard a sneeze, which sent Phantom scooting backwards, nearly dragging Charlie over. Mia and Alice turned to see an evergreen bush quivering, close behind the fencing where they were sitting.

"Rosie!" Mia called out. "Is that you?!"

The bush quivered again and Rosie stepped

out sheepishly, her cheeks bulging.

How long have you been hiding in there for?" Alice giggled as Charlie got Phantom back under control.

"Om, nt lng," Rosie mumbled with her mouth full, not looking at them but chewing quickly and swallowing. "Well, actually, a while. I got bored on lookout duty in the tack room. There was no sign of anyone, so I headed down here soon after you to watch Phantom, keeping out of sight so I didn't get rumbled. It was quite cosy in that bush, especially with these mini Yule logs to chomp on."

"Hang on," Mia said, deadly serious. "If you're down here, who was Beanie barking at on the yard a few minutes ago?"

They all looked at each other for half a second before Mia and Alice jumped down on the other side of the fence and sprinted, Rosie hot on their heels, towards to the yard. Rosie took a running leap at the back gate as Mia and Alice climbed it, but her foot slipped and she crashed noisily into the top of it and then tumbled down the other side.

"Are you okay?" Alice asked as Rosie untangled herself and rolled into an upright position. Mia held out her hand to help her up. Then they heard a clatter round the corner. Alice raced round, only to find the tack-room door swinging on its hinges, and Mia's pink body brush lying on the floor just outside. Alice ran to the front gate and jumped over it, then stood scanning each direction.

"Nothing," she reported to Rosie and Mia as they joined her. She climbed back over again just as hoof beats skittered onto the yard and Phantom appeared with Charlie. She led him back to his stable, then squealed as Hettie came shooting out of it just as they reached the door. Charlie held her breath, waiting for Phantom to explode, but to her surprise he just lowered his head instead, snorting and watching the sheep as she slowed to a halt in the middle of the yard, wondering where to go next.

"If Hettie's in the yard, my Pony Detective powers tell me that it *has* to be Megan. Again," Charlie said, bolting Phantom's stable before joining the others while Rosie persuaded a grumpy Hettie back to her field.

"Exactly. She must have waited until Rosie left the yard *unguarded*," Mia said, looking pointedly at Rosie, "then crept on. Only, Beanie gave her away."

Suddenly Rosie looked puzzled. "Hang on a sec, though. That doesn't add up," she said. "*I* heard Beanie barking playfully on the yard too, and thought it must have been at Mum or Dad, because he only barks like that at people he knows and likes..."

"And he doesn't like Megan," Alice said, realising what Rosie was getting at. "She was always tipping him off seats or squashing him when she sat down."

"So who was it, then?" Mia frowned.

"I'm going to ring Megan," Charlie said decisively, "so we can sort this out once and for all."

Charlie went into the tack room and looked for the number Megan had written down on a scrap of paper. Then she dialled it and switched on her speaker phone so the others could hear.

"Hello, is Megan there please?" Charlie asked politely, when Megan's dad answered.

"No, sorry, she's still out," he explained. "She's at the stables with the little bay pony she's got on loan. She should be back soon though.

Charlie thanked him and ended the call, looking round at the others.

"Proof!" she said. "It sounds like she's told her parents that she's got Pirate on loan!"

"And she's still determined to continue her plan to perfect him," Rosie added, "only now, she's gone undercover."

"And she's so desperate," Alice added, "that she even risked sneaking in here when she knew we were still nearby!"

"She probably saw Rosie heading for the paddocks then came over. I think we'll have to stay here again tomorrow so we can catch her out and put a stop to her creeping onto the yard all the time," Mia said seriously, as the others groaned at the idea of another day filled with tack cleaning. "Only this time, *Rosie*, we can't afford to make any mistakes."

Chapter Ten

ALICE'S mum drove slowly along the lane, the car's tyres crunching lightly on the inch-thick snow that had fallen the night before. She turned slowly into the drive for Blackberry Farm, and Charlie and Alice jumped out at the end, calling their goodbyes and thank-yous. Rosie and Mia were standing by the tack-room door, staring into the yard. They looked as if they'd seen a ghost.

"What's up?" Charlie asked anxiously, as she scrunched towards them with Alice.

Rosie didn't speak. She just pointed.

Alice and Charlie stood for a second, not knowing what they were supposed to be looking at. All the ponies were standing at their doors, except Phantom. Dancer scraped her hoof impatiently for her breakfast.

"I don't get it," Alice said, confused. "Everything looks the same as usual."

"There, on the ground," Mia whispered.

Charlie and Alice lowered their gaze. They both gasped, suddenly feeling goosebumps. There, clear in the light layer of snow, were hoof prints. They edged closer to get a better view. There were some more, little indistinct prints too, which looked as if they could have been made by Pumpkin, the yard cat.

"Those hoof prints lead from Pirate's stable," Charlie gasped, "to the gate, then back again!"

There was a scrape in the snow where it looked as if the gate had been pulled open.

"Are they definitely Pirate's hoof prints?" Alice asked.

Charlie nodded, feeling queasy. They were tiny – they could only belong to the smallest pony on the yard. "But both his bolts are still done up," she said.

"And there isn't a human footprint in sight." Alice shivered. There was a tiny strip untouched by snow around the edge of the stables, under the eaves, but it was too far away from the hoof prints for someone to have led Pirate out while walking beside him.

Charlie opened her little bay pony's door and he nudged her hard with his muzzle, his eyes bright, wanting his breakfast. Charlie ran her hands over his legs and turned back his rug; there wasn't a mark on him. She lifted one of his front hooves.

"I picked these out last night before we left," she said quietly, showing the others, her heart thudding, "but now they're full of mud and fern. The ground's frozen everywhere... apart from in the wood."

"He's been out of the yard," Rosie said, her eyes widening as Dancer nearly bashed her door off its hinges.

"Quick, we'd better feed the ponies first," Mia

said, taking a deep breath. "Then we can think about this."

They mixed together the chaff, pony nuts, garlic, chopped carrots and apples in silence, then walked back to hand out the buckets. Dancer nearly knocked her bucket out of Rosie's hand in her desperation to get to it. Charlie dropped one bucket into Pirate's stable, and he launched himself at it, lifting his near fore hoof as he tucked in greedily. As Charlie moved on and opened Phantom's door, she gasped, nearly dropping the bucket. Phantom always waited uneasily at the back of his stable until she'd left, and only then would he cautiously approach his feed. But this time he was standing quietly, his ears pricked and his eyes full of curiosity as he bent his head to the shape beneath him.

The others, hearing Charlie's gasp, rushed over and stood behind her, peering into the stable.

"Hettie!" Rosie exclaimed, then she slapped her hand over her mouth as Phantom jumped. She lowered her voice and he dropped his nose once more to the woolly ball standing triumphantly at his hooves. "Those smaller prints weren't Pumpkin's, they were hers! But how did *she* get in *there*?!"

"Do you reckon that Megan sneaked in overnight?" Alice asked. "I mean, I don't get how she could, if there weren't any footprints..."

"But Hettie being in is evidence that she was here," Mia puzzled. "Only – why put her in Phantom's box?"

"If Megan crept onto the yard after we'd all left," Charlie said, talking slowly while she thought things through, "and Hettie sneaked in with her, maybe it was easier for her to shove Hettie into one of the stables than try to get her back into the field."

"But how can it be her, or anyone else, in fact," Rosie asked, frightening herself, "if there wasn't a single footprint in the snow?"

The others stood stumped, and seriously spooked.

"I don't know," Mia eventually said, "but I think we might need to do a night-time watch if we're going to find out."

"There's no way I'm keeping a lookout on my own in the dark!" Rosie cried. "You're all going to have to stay with me – I'll ask Mum about a sleepover."

"Yes!" Alice said. "Then we can take it in turns to stay up and keep an eye on the yard."

"We *have* to work out what's going on here," Mia said. "But in the meantime, I vote we stay put. And I think Pirate should stay in his box under close guard all day."

"What about Hettie?" Rosie asked. "I'd take her out, but I'd rather not tackle her while she's being protected by Phantom the beast."

"You know what?" Charlie said, smiling for the first time that morning as she recalled the diary entry about Fable gaining confidence from her woolly companion, Molly. "I think it might just be the other way round. I don't suppose there's any chance your dad might let Hettie stay put, is there?"

Pirate stood miserably, watching Scout, Wish and Dancer being led to the field with their thick winter turnout rugs on. He whickered every time Charlie came near, his ears pricked hopefully, but he turned grumpy when she walked past telling him that he had to stay where they could keep an eye on him. She let herself into Phantom's stable, next door, and opened Fable's diary at the point where she'd finished reading the day before. Charlie settled herself quietly on the thick deep straw around the edge of the stable. Phantom stood in the far corner, but with Hettie planted firmly between them he looked less distrustful of Charlie. His back leg was relaxed and his ears had drooped slightly outwards. Charlie didn't feel she needed to tie him up.

At first she was aware of Pirate's restlessness in the next stable, and her reading was punctuated by his shrill whinnies to his stable mates.

But before long, she became lost to her surroundings, totally immersed in the other world created by Caitlin in the pages of the diary.

Charlie quickly lost track of time, reading silently for ages before she finally yawned and looked up. She felt her heart skip a beat. Phantom was half-dozing, his eyes soft. He shifted, but didn't start when she got up. She wanted to stroke him, but she kept her hand on the diary, gripping it firmly. Little steps, she told herself. She scraped back the bolt and let herself out of the stable. Pirate immediately whickered to her and paced his box, so Charlie went over and hugged his sturdy little upright neck, scratching his withers under the thick rug.

She walked to Wish's empty stable, where Rosie, Alice and Mia had spent the day with Beanie and Pumpkin, wrapped up in blankets reading old copies of *Pony Mad*, drinking hot chocolate from flasks and scoffing sandwiches and chocolate mini logs. That way they'd kept a close eye on the yard without making their presence visible, hoping Megan would sneak in. So far, though, the only creeping about had been done by the chickens clucking to and fro and the odd smoky-grey pigeon looking for loose feed in the yard.

Charlie sighed as she sat down with the others. She knew how much Pirate hated being cooped up, especially when his friends were out.

"It's only for one day," Mia reminded her as Rosie picked up the Christmas *Pony Mad* and started to flick through it. Alice was snuggled up next to Rosie, looking at the pages with her until they got to the classifieds.

Rosie was about to turn the page when Alice put out her hand to stop her, frowning. Part of the page was missing – just a tiny square from the bottom, and it was barely noticeable, but there was still a bit of pink highlighter on the page around the tear. Her mouth dropped open and she looked up at the others.

"You know that advert for the dressage pony we thought would suit Megan," she said quickly. "It's missing..."

The others looked over and gasped.

"Well none of us would've taken it," Charlie said, looking round at her friends, "which means..."

"It *has* to be Megan," Mia concluded with a frown. "When her dad said she was spending time with her bay loan pony, we just assumed he meant Pirate!"

"When he might have meant a different pony altogether." Rosie shivered. "But how do we know if that dressage pony is bay or not?"

"We call Rockland Riding School," Mia said quickly. "The pony was from there – has anyone got their number?"

Rosie ran to the cottage and came back with it. She rang it, but when the manager answered she suddenly went blank. She threw the phone like it was a hot potato to Mia, who caught it, put it on speakerphone and, rolling her eyes at Rosie, took over the conversation.

"Hi, I was wondering if the dressage pony advertised in *Pony Mad's* still up for loan?"

"Oh, I'm sorry, no. A young girl took him on a few days ago," the voice at the other end told them.

"I know it's an odd question," Mia continued, as the others held their breath, "but could you let me know what colour the pony is?"

"Of course!" the man laughed. "Mistral's a very handsome bright bay. Megan, his new rider, is over the moon with him."

Mia thanked the manager for the information, then ended the call and took a deep breath.

"It looks like this has just turned into a proper case, after all," she said to the others. A sudden chill gripped her and she pulled the blanket close.

The girls sat in stunned silence for a moment as the sky outside started to darken, until Charlie's phone buzzed, frightening them all half to death.

"It's Mrs Millar," she whispered before pressing the speakerphone button and answering, her heart still racing. Mia flipped to a new page in her notebook, ready to take notes for Charlie.

"Ah, Charlie, Mrs Millar here," Mrs Millar began, after Charlie had said hello. "I've done a bit of digging around and this is what I've found. You know some of it, but I'll go through it all anyway. So, Pixie's father bought Phantom in March this year. Before that, I had him on the yard for about eighteen months. He was a tricky horse but he settled after a while, helped by the friendship he got when Wish Me Luck arrived. Only, she was sold to your friend Mia pretty quickly, and he got fretful again after that.

"Now, I bought him off a woman called Liz, who was desperate to sell at any price. She'd got him as a four-year-old from a dealer, who promised that he was an amazing jumper. He was that all right, but he was a handful too, even by that age. Liz only had him a few months before deciding that she couldn't cope. The dealer refused to have him back, saying that he'd had Phantom since he was two and a half and he'd been backwards and forwards on trials the whole time. He'd been glad to get rid of him. While he was with me we took him right back to the start and he was going really nicely by the time he left. Spirited and quirky, always living on his nerves and fretting all the while, but so much talent. Not the friendliest, but then not every horse is, and I put that down to his chequered past."

Charlie glanced at Mia to check she was getting all of it down in her notebook. Mia nodded encouragingly.

Mrs Millar sighed. "Hmm, what next? Oh yes, that's it. Last night I managed to speak to the dealer that Liz bought him from. He picked Phantom up cheap from a woman called Ellie, who'd bought Phantom direct from his breeder. She was still fuming about it, apparently, convinced that the breeder had pulled a fast one, pretending the foal was older than he actually was. Ellie kept Phantom in a field for a couple of years but could never really get near him, he was too wild. So she sent him to the dealer, who then sold him on to Liz. I haven't managed to speak to the breeder yet, but I hear he's a bit of a slippery, unpleasant character. I've got his name here somewhere... now, where did I put it? Ah, yes, here it is, the breeder's name is Tim Leech."

Charlie gasped. She remembered the photo of Fable – she'd almost mistaken the black mare for Phantom. But Phantom *couldn't* be Fable's foal – her little colt had died! At least, that's what Tim Leech had told Caitlin all those years ago. Unless he'd lied to her.

Charlie sat stock still, stunned by Phantom's possible connection to Fable and Caitlin and the diary she held in her shaking hands. She cleared her throat and thanked Mrs Millar, then ended the call. Mia had written everything down in her notebook, but the words swam before Charlie's eyes and for a moment she couldn't move. Then she got up and walked to the stable next door. Phantom raised his head, and it was as if Charlie was seeing him for the first time: a gangly legged foal, wrenched from his mother too early, running scared ever since.

She heard the others emerge from Wish's stable, carrying out their blankets and mugs.

"Come on," Alice said. "Time to get the ponies in."

Chapter
Eleven

THEY brought in the other ponies and changed their rugs before dishing out their feeds.

"Right, we'd better start preparing for tonight," Mia announced after they'd had a quick sweep round and switched off the yard light. They'd debated whether to leave it on, but decided that they didn't want the routine to be different from normal, so they'd turned it off.

They went into the cottage and, over platefuls of piping-hot shepherd's pie, began to plan the evening ahead, deciding who was going to take which stints sitting at the big window seat in Rosie's bedroom that overlooked the stables. They discussed what reading material to take for when they were on lookout duty (Fable's diary and the

Christmas edition of *Pony Mad*), whether they should change into pyjamas and wear their clothes on top, and finally, what to do if someone *did* turn up.

As soon as they'd finished eating the girls raced upstairs, flying into Rosie's yellow bedroom, with its walls covered in pictures of Dancer, pony posters pulled from *Pony Mad* and wall charts about breeds, colours and markings. Her book shelves were stuffed with well-thumbed copies of every horse and pony book going. Mrs Honeycott had arranged a couple of blow-up beds and pulled in a spare mattress, all of which were piled with pillows, duvets and sleeping bags.

After they'd got settled on the beds, plumping for jeans and jumpers worn over pyjamas, Mia switched off the light, turned on her torch and pulled out her notebook. Rosie curled up under her duvet, and Alice sat next to Mia, while Charlie took up position on the window seat. With one hand she scooped up the curtain and looked out over the pitch-black yard; the only light was the soft glow coming from the downstairs windows of the cottage. In her other hand she held Fable's diary, now determined to finish it that night.

"Let's go through everything we've got so far," Mia said, flipping past the pages with 'Moonlight', 'Scout' and 'Runaway Pony' written at the top, until she came to the latest page, titled 'Pirate'.

Pumpkin jumped onto Charlie's lap as she nestled into her sleeping bag. She let the curtain fall, shutting out the cold, dark night, as Mia held the notebook under the beam of torchlight. Rosie and Alice shuffled closer to Mia as she began to read:

1 - Black hairs found in my pink body brush, several times - possibly one of the riders who came up to try Pirate out.

2 - Megan is the keenest of the lot and wants to turn Pirate into a dressage star. She pins up a training plan in the tack room.

3 - We try to put Megan off Pirate by showing
her an ad for a dressage pony for loan at
Rockland Riding School.

4 - Megan gets scared by Pirate's full-speed
gallop through the woods on her first
hack with him.

5 - Charlie tells Megan that she doesn't think
she should take Pirate on loan, but
Megan's already taken down her plan
from the tack-room wall - has her
decision been made?

6 - There are _more_ black hairs in my
grooming kit the following weekend,
and Pirate has been groomed and
has minty breath - is Megan sneaking
back in to continue with her plan?

7 - We leave a tail hair across the tack-room

door to see if anyone is coming onto the yard while we're out - we come back and it's broken!

8 - *Hettie's loose on the yard and Pirate's had his mane neatened, too.*

9 - *Next day, Beanie alerts us to the presence of a stranger (although it sounds like he knows AND LIKES the stranger - can't be Megan?).*

10 - *As we sneak up on the intruder Rosie trips over the gate, LOUDLY, and gives us away.*

11 - *My body brush is lying outside the tack room - someone's been in...*

12 - *Charlie calls Megan at home but she's out. Her Dad says she's spending time with her <u>bay</u> loan pony! Pirate???*

13 - *The next morning, there are hoof prints on the yard, but no footprints. Pirate's clean hooves have mud from the wood in them! AND, Hettie is in Phantom's box...?*

14 - *We discover that Megan has taken the dressage pony from Rockland Riding School on loan.*

15 - *So, if Megan isn't coming in here and messing about with Pirate and Hettie... who is???!!!*

"Someone who doesn't leave footprints," Alice said, spooking herself in the torch-lit bedroom as Mia finished reading out the last point. They talked over everything again and again, going round in circles without a single clue to follow, until they heard lights being turned off below them, footsteps on the stairs and lowered voices as Rosie's parents went to bed.

Charlie rested her head back against the wall, and played with Pumpkin's ears. She listened while the others whispered about what might be going on for what felt like ages, until the house fell silent. Suddenly, Charlie remembered that she was meant to be keeping an eye on the yard. She pulled back the curtain to peep behind it. A bright white moon lit up the sky, fading in and out as silver-edged clouds drifted slowly over its surface. An instant chill gripped her.

"Pirate's stable door!" she squeaked. "It's open!"

Suddenly the room burst into life as everyone unzipped their sleeping bags and rushed to the window.

"I can't see him anywhere!" Charlie panicked, pressed up against the window and searching desperately as a larger cloud drifted across the moon.

"I can't see my socks, either," Rosie muttered, wishing now that she'd kept them on. She hopped over to the light just as Mia pointed out of the window.

"There, heading down between the paddocks!"

Charlie peered. She could only just see Pirate's outline in the shadows thrown by the moon.

At that very second Rosie reached the light. Alice turned and squealed at her to stop, but it was too late. The room was flooded with light, suddenly reflecting Charlie and Mia's faces back at them in the glass until Alice raced over and flicked it off again.

"I've lost him!" Charlie whispered urgently, her eyes taking a while to adjust.

"Quick, let's go," Mia said as Rosie grabbed her socks and pulled them on. They hurriedly crept down the stairs, trying not to trip in the dark. They grabbed Mr Honeycott's huge torch from its position by the front door, scraped the key in the lock and tumbled out into the freezing air. Scout came to the front of his stable, blinking sleepily as the girls sprinted across the yard and through the open gate, the beam from the torch bobbing in front of them.

Rosie swept the path ahead with the light, then she suddenly caught sight of a shadowy movement by the edge of the trees and dropped the torch in fright. Charlie called Pirate's name in a wobbly voice, as loud as she dared, and the next second they heard trotting hooves. The small bay pony emerged out of the dark and pulled up in front of them. Charlie grabbed his headcollar. The lead rein had been moved and was clipped onto the side again. She noticed that his ears were pricked and his eyes were shining; he looked happy. Rosie picked up the torch and shone it into the entrance of the woods.

"I can't see anything," Mia shivered. "Do you think we should go in...?"

"No way!" Rosie squeaked, grabbing Alice's arm.

"I'm with Rosie. I seriously think we should get back – now!" Alice whispered, her legs like jelly as they stood in the eerie, dark silence of the chill night air.

Without another word they turned and walked back to the yard, getting faster and faster until they were practically running. As Charlie trotted Pirate into his stable she saw that his top rug had been taken off and bundled in a corner, leaving him with just his thinner, fleecy under-rug.

Once Pirate was settled the Pony Detectives walked quickly across the yard back to the house, rushing through the door and turning the key with shaking fingers. They flew upstairs as quietly as possible, pulled off their outdoor clothes and collapsed onto their beds, all except for Charlie, who snuggled down into her nest on the window seat.

"So did you see anyone riding Pirate?" Rosie whispered loudly, her heart still thumping.

"It was too dark to see much," Mia whispered back, her voice shaking. "But I... I couldn't be sure about seeing anyone up there."

"No footprints, no rider..." Rosie squeaked, flicking on the torch and holding it under her chin as she pulled a ghoulish face right next to Alice.

"Stop it, Rosie!" Alice squealed, nearly tumbling off the side of her blow-up bed. As Rosie collapsed into nervous giggles, Mia muttered about them needing to take it seriously. The door creaked open and Mia leaped onto Rosie's bed, terrified. Rosie jumped too, then snorted with silent laughter as Pumpkin padded into the bedroom.

He joined Charlie in the window seat, purring loudly. He rubbed his head against her chin as she picked up the diary and put one arm around him, partly to keep warm, and partly because he made her feel less spooked. As her heart continued to pound, she decided to finish the diary, too filled with nervous excitement and questions to sleep. She could hear the others' whispered conversations start to fade, interrupted by yawns. Once the room had fallen silent she switched on her torch. She flicked through the earlier entries, then turned to the last pages and began to read.

Fable has turned a corner! Today, for the first time ever, she whinnied to me as I stepped out of my back door and walked to her paddock! Neve was so excited too, and before I could stop her, she wriggled under the fence to see Fable. I froze, but Fable stayed quiet, just dipping her muzzle and blowing gently on Neve's head, rustling her hair. Neve was over the moon, she hasn't stopped talking about it since. She wanted to mark the occasion so we went for a walk to Whispering Bridge as a celebration, all three of us, so Neve could make a wish. And for the first time, Fable walked beside me and Neve, without pulling away or nipping.

She sniffed the bushes and the ground as we went - she even stepped into the water to cool her legs. Her ears were pricked, she looked happy. I held Neve's hand as she climbed onto the rocks and dropped her penny in the stream, and heard her whispered wish - that Fable would always be as happy as she looked today. It was perfect.

I really think this is the end of one chapter and the start of another in Fable's life. I'm going to make sure that this and every chapter from now on is the happiest she could wish for... I can't wait for tomorrow and all that it will bring!

Charlie stared at the entry, her heart aching – she knew that just hours later, Fable would be dead, and Caitlin and Neve's world would be shattered. She turned the page, but there were no more entries. Charlie sighed, wondering if what came next had been just too painful to write about. Then she noticed ruffles of jagged paper running down the inside of the diary. She looked closer, then realised that the last few pages had been torn out.

Charlie frowned and leaned back against the wall, whispering to Pumpkin that she would text Fran Hope in the morning to thank her and ask if she knew where the last pages were. Charlie quietly slid down from the window seat, stepped over a sleeping Alice and placed the diary on Rosie's bedside table. Then she climbed back up and wrapped herself in sleeping bag and duvet. Exhausted, her tired eyes closed and she drifted into a restless sleep just as fat, heavy snowflakes began to dance beyond the window.

Chapter
Twelve

CHARLIE woke stiffly, cramped in the window seat. She stretched and moved the curtain back to peep out. A deep, bright white carpet of snow had settled, covering everything she could see. The yellowy grey clouds in the sky sat low, thick flurries of snowflakes falling solidly. She sat up, suddenly remembering what had happened the night before, and peered at Pirate's stable. With a burst of relief she realised that his stable door was still closed. Pumpkin blinked up at her and Charlie smiled, reaching for her mobile.

"Thanks for reminding me," she said quietly as she texted Fran Hope to ask about the diary.

When the text had sent, Charlie slid out from under her duvet and the cosily warm sleeping bag, shivering at once as she hastily pulled on her thick jumper and the jeans by her side.

"Wake up!" she said, nudging Alice's bed as she tugged on her fleecy socks. Alice stirred and sat up, yawning.

"What's the rush?" she asked in a croaky voice.

"Snow!" Charlie whispered back. "And I want to see if there are any clues from last night."

Mia sat up, looking as immaculate and neat as when she went to bed the night before. Charlie's hair was poking out in every direction, Alice had forgotten to take out her hairband and now half of her mousey brown ponytail was in it and half was out. Rosie, as Alice shook her, sat up with her blonde hair sticking up like a haystack.

"If you're going clue-hunting," Mia said, picking up her notebook, "we're coming too. Come on, Rosie."

Rosie groaned loudly, slinking back under her duvet cover until Charlie told her that it had snowed. Hearing that, Rosie rolled out of bed, sending Beanie sliding off the duvet with a low gruffle. Then she tripped over Alice's bed in her attempt to get to the window, still half asleep.

"Er, aren't any clues going to be completely buried in snow by now?" she asked, rubbing her eyes and squinting at the brightness outside.

"You've got a point," Mia agreed, starting to smile. "But we'd better look anyway, just in case."

The others got dressed quickly, pulling on as many layers as they could find to keep out the cold, then they all flew downstairs, in a rush to feed the ponies. They flung open the back door and ran outside, twirling in the falling flakes. Rosie stuck out her tongue to catch some as she and the girls fluffed into the snow. It already came up to their ankles, and they sprayed it around as they slipped and slid their way over the gate. There were already large footprints in the snow from where Mr Honeycott and Rosie's older brother, Will, had set off to check the sheep in the fields near the lane and scatter some extra hay so they had enough to eat. In the yard, all the ponies except Phantom were standing at the front of their stables whickering a hungry greeting. Charlie leaned over Phantom's door.

"Morning," she said quietly, smiling at him. The black horse stood at the back of his stable as usual, but this time the atmosphere inside wasn't simmering with fear and distrust. Instead, a quiet stillness hung in the air, with a very contented and cosy-looking Hettie, standing knee-deep in straw, keeping the black horse company.

The girls had fed the ponies and were about to disappear down to the woods, when Mrs Honeycott called them back inside to have some orange juice and porridge drizzled with honey before they went any further. They ate at breakneck speed, blowing loudly on each spoonful before shovelling and slurping it down, until they'd finished. Then they raced to the entrance of the woods.

"Too much snow," Rosie declared, as Alice

started to move it about, using her foot as a makeshift shovel.

At that second Charlie's phone beeped. She pulled it out of her pocket and read the text.

"It's from Fran Hope," she said, suddenly feeling an icy finger run down her spine.

"What does it say?" Mia asked, seeing Charlie go pale.

"I finished the diary last night and there were some pages missing at the back," Charlie explained, "so I texted first thing this morning to thank Fran for bringing it round and to ask if she knew where they were."

"And?" Rosie and Alice asked together, impatient.

"She says that she'd forgotten all about the diary," Charlie shivered. "In fact, she'd forgotten to even look for it. Which means that if *she* didn't find Fable's diary, she couldn't have been the one who dropped it round..."

Just then, Rosie's mobile rang, and the four

Pony Detectives leaped out of their skins, their hearts thudding. Rosie checked the flashing screen and frowned as she answered it.

"Dad?" she said, looking at the others with widening eyes as she listened in silence for a moment. "No, we haven't seen her... she's never been to the yard... Okay, we'll have a think."

"What's up?" Mia asked, seeing from Rosie's expression that something serious had happened.

"It's Neve," Rosie explained quickly. "Her grandparents just bumped into Dad and Will in the village. Apparently they had a row with Neve last night after they told her that she'd definitely be staying in England. They know Neve's been really unhappy, so they told her that they'd arranged to move into the annexe at Hope Farm, where she used to live with her mum. They wanted to move somewhere smaller anyway, because Mr McCuthers has retired, and they thought that moving back to her old house would make Neve happy. Only, it seems to have made things worse. She said she'd never go there and stormed off to bed. They left her to it, but when they checked this morning her room was empty and she'd taken a bag full of clothes and stuff! It sounds like she's run away!"

The girls gasped.

"Where would she have headed?" Mia asked.

"That's what Dad said Mr and Mrs McCuthers have been trying to figure out," Rosie said. "Dad said he'd ask us if we might know."

The girls stood in the heavily falling snow, silent for a moment.

"The only place we've seen her is the woods," Charlie said, biting her lip and concentrating hard. She looked up and scoured the trees, but with the snow still coming down it was hard to see far through them.

"She doesn't really know anywhere else, does she?" Mia said, racking her brains.

Suddenly Alice gasped.

"But she does though, doesn't she?" she said.

"She knows Whispering Bridge!"

"Of course!" Mia exclaimed. "She went there with her mum and Fable! And I told her how to find it again, too! It might be worth going there to check."

The Pony Detectives all looked at each other, panicking as they pictured the rushing, freezing water, the tumbledown bridge and the slippery rocks on the banks, which would now be hidden by the snow.

"I'd better tell Dad," Rosie said grimly. "But the trouble is the only tracks leading to it are way too narrow and the trees are too dense to drive any kind of Jeep down. Worse still, it'll take ages for anyone to follow her on foot – she's had a serious head start!"

The girls stood for a moment, then Charlie took a deep breath. "There is another option," she said, turning back to the yard and racing towards the back gate.

The others jogged after her and got there just

as Charlie emerged from the tack room, Phantom's tack trailing from her arm as she yanked on her riding hat.

"No way, Charlie!" Rosie squeaked. "Are you mad?"

"You're banned from riding Phantom, remember?" Mia said desperately, her voice shaking. Charlie stopped by Phantom's box and turned round.

"I know, and Mum will probably kill me for doing this, if Phantom doesn't first," Charlie explained, feeling the butterflies going wild inside her. "But he's the fastest horse here by miles, and if I take the short cut I might get there in time to head Neve off. Phantom's the best chance she has, if that's where she's gone."

Charlie slid into Phantom's stable, her shaking hands gripping the tack.

The black horse raised his head away from her but she took the headcollar as firmly as she could, knowing that every second might count.

She looked at Phantom, the awesome, powerful black horse in front of her, and tried to picture the fearful, lost little foal inside, so that she could get her own fear under control. If she was going to get back on top of him after her last fall, she knew that it would take every ounce of her courage. And she'd need the same from Phantom in return. Phantom seemed to sense the urgency, and he stood stock still, his ears half back as Charlie fumbled with the buckles and keepers, her heart racing. She fastened her hat, pushing it hard onto her head.

As she led Phantom out into the swirling snow he towered above her, snorting as he high-stepped into the yard. Rosie shut his stable door before Hettie could escape, and Mia legged Charlie up. Charlie was so tense and rigid that she almost tipped right over the other side of the saddle.

Suddenly Alice shot off to the tack room, slipping on the snow.

"I'm going to check the long route," she said,

coming out holding her tack, "just in case Neve is still following the brook. Have you got your mobile?"

Charlie nodded and tightened the girth as Phantom skittered beneath her.

"Me and Rosie had better stay, in case Neve doesn't head for the bridge and turns up here instead," Mia said as she nervously held the black horse's reins. She looked up, her face etched with worry. "Take it steady, Charlie, and be careful!"

Mia let go of the reins and Charlie turned Phantom, her chest tight and her breath shallow. Even in the few days since she'd stopped riding him, she'd forgotten how high up she was and how light Phantom was on his hooves. He tossed his head at the snow and snorted, fretful and anxious. Charlie glanced over at Pirate's familiar little face, looking at her from over the stable door, and wished more than ever that she was setting out on her steadfast, totally trustworthy friend.

For a second Charlie wondered if she should abandon her mission now, while she still could. Then she thought of Neve, feeling miles from home, desolate after losing everything – her mum, her home, her friends and the ponies at the rescue yard in Ireland. She could be making her way to Whispering Bridge at that very moment, and if she tried to step onto the stones to make a wish... Without thinking, Charlie put her legs to Phantom's side. The black horse flattened his ears and the next second he half-reared, kicking out a front hoof. Charlie leaned into him, her eyes almost shut, then Phantom plunged forward and they flew out of the yard in a swirl of snow and thundering hooves.

Chapter Thirteen

"STEADY, Phantom," Charlie whispered, her voice tense as they skidded out of the yard and trotted down the path between the two paddocks. She could barely see as the snow blustered into her eyes. Phantom struggled to find his footing over the rutted, frozen ground, tripping twice in quick succession and almost unseating Charlie. She stood up in her stirrups and grabbed a handful of Phantom's silky black mane.

As soon as he was on the woodland path, he surged forward like a rocket. Charlie tightened her grip on his mane as his stride got faster and faster. She narrowed her eyes, blinking away the snow as the speed took her breath from her. Feeling his huge stride powering beneath her as they careered along the bridleway, she knew that it was Phantom who was in charge, barely aware of her presence on his back.

Up ahead was a fork in the path – the right one would take her on the short cut to Whispering Bridge, the left one on the long route. She pressed her left leg and touched the right rein to turn Phantom towards the short cut. At once he flung up his head, his mane in Charlie's face, plunging ahead without turning and losing his rhythm. Great white plumes of breath fired from his flaring nostrils as they flew faster along the path, heading for the trees dead ahead in the centre of the fork.

Charlie panicked, unable to react. "Turn, Phantom, turn!" Charlie cried. She felt totally powerless, almost paralysed by fear and frustration, and wondering why she'd thought for even a second that she could control a horse like Phantom. Hot tears stung her frozen cheeks, but as she saw the trees racing towards her she realised that she couldn't give up: she *had* to get to the bridge. She sat down in the saddle and made one last desperate attempt to turn Phantom. She gave him a sharp, determined kick with her left leg. Suddenly, Phantom's ears flickered back and at the last second he skidded to the right, a hind hoof nearly slipping out behind him. Charlie toppled to the left, saw the ground get suddenly closer, then hauled herself back into the saddle. Somehow, she was still on board and now they were flashing through the woods, Charlie wiping her eyes with the back of her glove to see, and trying to slow Phantom and steer him round the twisting path. The first few times he ignored her, fighting for his head and only just making the bend in time. But after a few corners his ears started to flicker, and she felt him sink back slightly into his haunches to steady himself for each one.

"Good boy!" Charlie cried, patting him without taking her hands off the reins. Whenever there was a straight path, Charlie leaned forward and urged the black horse on. Phantom responded, stretching his head, his neck down and lengthening his stride, with his silky mane flowing into Charlie's face as she tucked low over him.

His ears flickered backwards and forwards at the sound of her voice as she reassured him. She talked softly, to calm herself down as much as to calm the black horse as they tackled tangled turn after twisting bend. They flew over snow-laden branches that had fallen across the path, Phantom barely breaking his stride as Charlie softened her hands and tucked forward.

Galloping up the final long slope before the bridge, she crouched low over Phantom's withers, urging him on. He responded by dipping his neck further, his legs pumping faster. She knew that if her aching lungs were anything to go by, his must be burning too. Near the top of the slope she felt his stride start to labour and shorten beneath her, and she eased him up slightly, patting his sweating neck.

"Nearly there," she whispered. "Just this bend at the top, then it's a straight downhill path to the stream."

They reached the bend and cantered round. Charlie's heart leaped into her throat. There, blocking the path in front of them, was a huge fallen tree, its roughened, snow-decked trunk vast and broad. The path fell away so steeply on the other side that it looked as if it ended with the trunk and there was nothing beyond but air.

Charlie sat upright, squeezing hard on her reins. Phantom, already tiring, skidded to a sliding halt at the base of the trunk, his muzzle bumping into it. Charlie slipped up his neck, nearly flying off sideways. She clung on, and then shuffled back – but not before she spotted a red coat in the distance.

"Neve!" Charlie shouted, cupping her hands around her mouth. Her cry bounced off the trees, whipped back by the icy wind as Phantom pranced restlessly, his sides heaving, beneath her.

Neve didn't look round: she didn't even hear. Charlie glanced over at both sides of the path. The tangled thickets of bushes were too dense for her to attempt to get through. But she couldn't abandon Phantom up there on the path by himself – she couldn't risk him wandering off. There was only one way to get to the other side. They'd have to jump it.

"We don't have a choice, Phantom," Charlie whispered, trying not to think about the fact that it was bigger than anything she'd ever jumped before. She turned Phantom away from the trunk, jogging him for a few strides, then turned again, taking a deep breath and squeezing her legs to his sides.

The black horse responded at once, bouncing forward into a strong canter. He locked onto the trunk and lowered his head, but in the last stride he faltered. Charlie knew that it must look to him as if she was asking him to jump off the edge of the earth, but she clamped her legs to his sides, squeezing tighter. His ears flickered, and Charlie felt her heart flip: he was going to jump like she'd asked him, no matter what was on the other side. In that instant she realised that the black horse trusted her.

Phantom launched himself into the air with a grunt, the crest of his neck knocking Charlie upwards. Her chin scraped on his mane as she folded forwards, trying desperately to stay in balance. He tucked up his hooves, suspended for what felt like for ever, before flicking them out and plunging to the ground on the other side. Charlie's breath left her as he knuckled forward, and she leaned back, letting the reins slip through her fingers but not letting them go completely. Phantom scooped back up, then in the next stride they were skidding downhill, sending the powdery snow flying in every direction.

"Well *done* Phantom! Good boy!" Charlie cried, patting his neck as she scanned the stream's edge. Then she saw Neve, her arms circling wildly as she tried to balance on the rocks by the edge of the stream. As Charlie watched what happened next, it was as if things were suddenly in slow motion. Neve's foot slipped from under her, and she plunged into the water.

ʊ ʊ ʊ ʊ

Charlie leaped off Phantom and raced to the water's edge.

"Neve!" she cried, looking around desperately for her.

At that second, Neve bobbed back up, coughing and spluttering.

Charlie could see her stumbling in the rushing current, which was waist-height and icy cold. Neve's lips already looked blue and she was shivering all over, but her eyes were fixed on the black horse.

"Fable?" she whispered.

"It's not Fable," Charlie replied, trying to

work out how to get Neve out of the water. "It's Phantom."

"Oh, Fable..." Neve said, looking up, disorientated for a second before trying to scramble out. But then she slid back off the slippery rocks, almost submerging beneath the water.

"Neve! Listen to me! Walk this way a bit," Charlie shouted urgently, pointing up the stream, further away from the bridge. "The bank's less steep there."

Neve tried to walk against the current of the flowing water, her teeth chattering and her clothes soaked and heavy. They weighed her down, so that every tiny step took for ever. Charlie could see that Neve was already tiring. She panicked, looking round. Then she saw Phantom, standing a few steps off, his neck flecked with sweat.

Charlie rushed up to him and took the reins over his head. "Just one more effort, I promise," she whispered as she started to lead him closer to the stream. He shied backwards from the water for a couple of strides before stopping stock still, his head raised, snorting through his blood-red, flaring nostrils. At the moment that she realised Phantom was scared, Charlie also realised that all her fear of the black horse had disappeared. She moved to his shoulder and stroked his neck, then walked him on again. Nervously, he took a step forward, keeping close to Charlie's shoulder until he was near to the edge. Charlie flung the reins to Neve. She grabbed them with shaking, numb hands, as Charlie turned and took hold of Phantom's bridle.

"Walk on," Charlie said, clicking and taking a step along the riverbank, encouraging her horse to follow. Phantom hesitated, panicking momentarily as he first felt the pull of Neve's weight on his reins. They slipped through Neve's fingers, but she kept hold. Charlie patted Phantom, then asked again. This time he sunk into his hindquarters and pushed off them, pausing every couple of steps before starting again as Charlie either 'whoa-ed' or clicked, responding to her even though he was unsure. Slowly, he helped pull Neve out of the water to the shallower ledge of the bank, then Charlie rushed to reach out her hand to help haul Neve the rest of the way.

Neve collapsed on a tree stump. Charlie pulled off her own jacket and wrapped it around Neve's narrow shoulders, reaching quickly for her mobile phone.

"Everyone's running round like mad trying to find you," Charlie told her. She looked at Neve's pale, troubled face, then texted Mia, Rosie and Alice:

**Found Neve at Whispering Bridge –
wet but safe.**

She got a text back almost instantly from Mia:

**Phew!! Mr Honeycott on way with Will.
They've got blankets.**

Neve looked away. "I told my nan and granddad I didn't want to stay, but they wouldn't listen," she said in a quiet, shivery voice. "I just want everything to go back to how it was. I... I came here and made my wish, but then I slipped and fell into the water. Then I heard hoofbeats and looked up and saw... well, I just thought, somehow, my wish had come true..."

Neve looked at the black horse with a longing that made Charlie's heart ache. At that moment a voice called out, echoing through the silence of the woods. Charlie recognised it at once.

"Alice!" she shouted back. "Down here!"

A grey shape appeared out of the snow as Scout and Alice emerged at the brow of the hill, which led down to the stream from the long route. Alice gasped, stopping at the bank as she saw Neve sitting there soaked and chilled, her face paler than ever.

"Can Neve ride back with you?" Charlie asked. "Phantom's too tired to be ridden."

"'Course," Alice replied, shuffling back in the saddle. Neve stood shakily and squelched towards Scout. Charlie helped her haul her wellies off, tipping out the water before putting them back on. Alice dragged off her own jacket for Neve to add on top of Charlie's, then Charlie legged Neve up so that she was sat in front of Alice, to soak up what extra warmth she could.

"Mr Honeycott and Will are on their way," Charlie said, trying to smile. She cupped her hands in front of her mouth and blew into them. "They didn't set out that long ago but they're bringing blankets."

Alice nodded, looking down at Charlie, who was starting to shiver without her jacket to keep out the icy chill.

"Are you sure you're going to be okay walking back?" Alice frowned as she turned Scout towards the slope. "It'll take ages, and it might be a while before we bump into Will and Mr Honeycott."

Charlie nodded. However tired she might be,

she could see that Phantom was weary and it would be kinder to lead him. "He's done enough for today. You can go ahead if you want to – I don't mind."

Alice shook her head. "No way. We'll go back together even if it takes longer," she replied decisively. "I'm not leaving you, not like that."

Charlie smiled gratefully and passed Neve's bag to Alice. Alice slung it over one shoulder. Then Charlie turned to Phantom, who stood with his head low, his sides still heaving and steam rising up off his neck. As she walked towards him, she just hoped that he would be okay too.

"Come on, boy," she said quietly, picking up his reins and walking him over to Alice. He set off stiffly, his muzzle at Charlie's elbow.

She scrunched in the snow beside him, one hand resting on his neck, as much for her as for him. Ahead of her Scout strode on purposefully, his stocky frame easily carrying Alice and Neve. They took the long path back; it wasn't full of twists and turns like the short cut, and it seemed to take for ever. Everything around them was silent except for Scout and Phantom's rhythmical hoofbeats, disrupted occasionally as Phantom wearily tripped over the odd tree root hidden by the snow. Then Charlie heard a groaning creak above her. She looked up, seeing the grey sky criss-crossed with branches. Something creaked again, more loudly this time; she glanced up just in time to see an old, gnarled branch split under the weight of the snow.

"Alice – look out!" Charlie cried. Alice instinctively pressed her legs to Scout's sides. Her grey pony scooted forwards, but Phantom had nowhere to go and he started, his ears flat back just as the branch swung down, cracking onto his hindquarters, its dead, spiky twigs catching his tail. Phantom's head flew up, and even though he was tired he exploded upwards and forward, pulling Charlie off her feet as her frozen fingers couldn't let go of the reins fast enough.

She stumbled to the ground, her arm hitting a tree root and the weight of her body landing on top.

"Steady!" Charlie heard Alice cry, and she looked up to see Phantom crashing past Scout, almost knocking Alice out of the saddle. She watched helplessly as Phantom flew up the path ahead, bucking with every stride as the branch remained caught in his tail. Suddenly it was dislodged and he bolted, scared into flight, his reins caught over his near foreleg.

Charlie lay in the icy snow, unable to breathe for a second. Alice got a spooked Scout under control and jogged him back to where her friend was lying.

"Are you hurt?" Alice asked anxiously. Charlie managed to sit up shakily. Shooting pains ran up her wrist.

"I... I'm not sure," Charlie said shakily. "My arm's pretty painful."

As Charlie dizzily tried to stand, Alice felt her

eyes well up, frightened and unsure what to do next. She didn't want to leave her friend, but she didn't know how to get her home, either. On top of that, Neve was sitting in front of her, shivering violently and Alice knew she couldn't dither for long.

"Maybe we should ride on until we find Mr Honeycott and Will?" Neve suggested through chattering teeth, looking back over her shoulder.

"Good idea," Alice said in a rush, scrabbling to pull her mobile phone from her pocket. "I'll call them too, so they know to take the long path and to hurry. Charlie – are you okay to stay here while we carry on?"

Charlie nodded, feeling too sick to move. With one last look Alice turned and squeezed Scout into a steady canter, reins in one hand, her mobile pressed to her ear. Charlie watched as Scout's dappled grey rump merged into the falling snow and disappeared around a turn in the path.

Charlie sat for a while in the heavy silence of

the woods, waiting for her stomach to stop churning. Then she stood up. It felt as if she'd been alone for ages, and her legs were leaden as she started to walk slowly up the path. She hadn't got far when she heard shouts and cries ahead. She looked up and saw Mr Honeycott and Will running towards her.

"There you are!" Mr Honeycott puffed, looking seriously relieved as he reached her side and slid to a halt. "We set out as soon as Alice called – then Phantom galloped round a bend out of nowhere and almost knocked us flying! We didn't know what to expect until we met Alice and Neve further up the track and they told us what had happened."

"Is Phantom…" Charlie asked. She was unable to finish, her voice coming out in a croak as she cradled her left wrist.

"I've just called Rosie. Phantom's found his way back to the stables and they're seeing to him," Will added as Mr Honeycott wrapped a blanket around Charlie's shoulders. "But right now we need to concentrate on getting you home. That arm looks pretty sore."

"It wasn't Phantom's fault," Charlie said in a voice that sounded miles away. She was so cold, so tired, and her wrist was throbbing. She tried to ask how Neve was, but she couldn't get the words out. The woods started to blur in front of her, then everything went black.

Chapter Fourteen

Charlie had only fainted for a few moments. She came to, and leaned on Mr Honeycott and Will as they slowly made their way back to the yard. As they approached, Alice, Rosie and Mia rushed down between the paddocks to meet them.

"You better get straight inside and have that arm checked," Mr Honeycott said as the girls fussed over their friend and filled her in on Neve, who was in trouble with everyone for running away, but apart from that, was okay. She had been whipped off to Rosie's bedroom for a sugar-filled hot chocolate and a change of clothes. Then they gave Charlie the news about Phantom, who'd reached the yard before she had. A second later Mrs Honeycott came running over with a worried look on her face, telling Charlie that she'd called her mother and announcing that she herself was first-aid trained and had the bandages out and ready.

"Now, come on, Charlie – inside," she said.

"I've got to check on Phantom first," Charlie insisted, ignoring Mrs Honeycott's protests and trudging over on tired legs to Phantom's box, the others around her.

She let herself in. Hettie was standing protectively in front of Phantom. Charlie's face fell when she saw him – his head and neck were low and he was unsettled, shifting his weight between his back hooves and leaving his haynet untouched.

"I've put a sweat rug on under his lightest stable rug," Mia told her. "And he's had a bit of a drink, but we didn't give him loads after he'd done so much as we didn't want to risk giving him colic."

Charlie nodded her thanks, biting her lower lip to stop it wobbling.

"He was as good as gold," Rosie continued, looking hesitantly at the others, "which we thought was highly suspicious, so Alice called the new vet – the one that's taken over from Mr McCuthers."

"He's on his way, just to check him over," Alice added quickly, trying to smile reassuringly and failing. Charlie watched as her black horse's large, dark eyes stared ahead at the wooden stable wall, not caring, for the first time, that she was standing near him. Alice had done the right thing: she knew as well as they did that something looked very wrong.

U U U U

"It's just badly bruised," Mrs Honeycott announced, after the rest of the Pony Detectives had finally managed to usher Charlie away from Phantom's stable and up to bed. Neve, wearing a collection of Rosie's colourful knitted jumpers, slipped quietly from the room and Charlie sank, exhausted, into Rosie's bed. The girls tucked her under the duvet and propped her up on a huge pile of pillows.

Just as they finished, the door opened and Charlie's mum came into the room. Her face was full of concern, made worse when she saw the crisp white bandage wound round Charlie's wrist.

"We'll leave you to it," Mrs Honeycott said, stepping out of the room. Mia beckoned to the others and they hurried out too.

Charlie's mum sat on the bed and carefully hugged Charlie. After checking she was okay, Charlie's mum sighed. "I've called Pixie, and Mrs Millar," she said gently. "I'm sorry darling, but Pixie's agreed it's time for Mrs Millar to start looking for a new buyer for Phantom." As Charlie started to protest, her mum held up her hand. "He's had his last chance, Charlie, he has to go. He's just too dangerous. You should never have been on him in the first place today, in case you'd forgotten. Mrs Millar's collecting him at lunchtime tomorrow."

There was a faint creak on the landing outside the room followed by the sound of light footsteps creeping down the stairs. Hot tears sprang to Charlie's eyes.

"But he did everything I asked of him!" she gulped. "It wasn't his fault that I hurt my wrist! I know he spooked and bolted when the branch hit him, but that wasn't his fault – he was scared! And we found out that he was taken away from his mother too early, and he's been moved around to far too many homes, *and* he's never had the chance to settle in any of them."

"Sweetheart, that's very sad," Charlie's mum sighed, "but it still doesn't stop him being untrustworthy and unsafe."

"He just needs time and love," Charlie cried. "We *can't* get rid of him now! And he's improved so much since I got advice from..."

"Advice?" Charlie's mum asked, frowning. "Who from?"

"I... I'm not sure," Charlie replied, looking

down at her wrist. "But I've been reading this diary that was dropped off here..."

"A diary? Whose diary? Who dropped it off?" Her mum frowned.

"Well, I don't exactly know," Charlie winced, sitting up and looking round Rosie's bedroom. "I left it here last night but it... it's disappeared."

"Disappearing diaries that get dropped off by magic?" her mum said, shaking her head. "No, my mind's made up. Phantom goes tomorrow."

Charlie tried to protest but her voice got stuck in her throat. She heard the others calling out goodbye to Neve and then thudding footsteps as they climbed the stairs.

"Now, come on. I should get you home."

"There's no way I'm leaving Phantom tonight," Charlie said defiantly. "I know it's Christmas Eve tomorrow but I've got to be here in case he needs me. I haven't even seen the vet yet – is he still here?"

"He was leaving as I arrived," her mum said

with a sigh. "He said that Phantom's pretty exhausted and that someone needs to keep an eye on him, in case anything changes. In your state I don't think that someone should be you."

"We're all staying, if that helps?" Mia suggested, cheekily popping her head round the door. "We've checked with our parents and it's okay, so we can keep an eye on Phantom *and* Charlie."

Alice and Rosie crept in behind her, nodding.

"Well, only if it's okay with Rosie's parents," Charlie's mum said tentatively.

"Already asked," Rosie beamed, "and they've said it's okay."

"Well, all right then," Charlie's mum replied, heading to the door, "but make sure you rest well today, and it doesn't change anything about tomorrow. Mrs Millar's coming with her horsebox, and that's final."

Charlie collapsed back against the pillows, exhausted and defeated, her eyes filling with tears.

Mia sat in the window seat, looking out over the yard. The front door of the cottage opened and Neve appeared, still bundled up in Rosie's jumpers, with plastic bags inside her wellies to keep her feet dry, and wrapped in thick blankets. Mr and Mrs McCuthers walked with her. Mia watched as Neve looked across the yard, then climbed into the back seat of a car that was parked as if it had been left in a hurry. Beanie followed her, hopping over the snow in little leaps, bouncing up and down at Neve's side. As the engine stirred and the car began to move off slowly, wheels slipping on the snow towards the drive, Beanie raced after it as far as the tall hedge then trotted back to the house, ducking back into the warmth.

Mia chewed her lip, frowning, as Rosie and Alice tried to come up with a plan to save Phantom. Charlie closed her eyes, not wanting to talk. She knew that no words could stop the growing ache she felt inside at the thought of losing Phantom, just when she'd started to understand him. She also finally understood a tiny bit of the heartache that Neve must have felt since she'd come to England, after losing almost every thing she cared about.

Chapter Fifteen

Charlie drifted in and out of sleep all afternoon before finally waking up properly to find the room had grown dark. Her wrist ached as she sat up awkwardly. She switched on the bedside lamp and saw a note scrawled by Rosie propped up against it.

Sorting out the ponies' feeds and rugs, back soon with pizza! Yum!!

Charlie smiled at the note then struggled up, feeling stiff all over. A moment later there was a snuffle at the door and Beanie's alert little face appeared. He jumped up on the bed and shoved his wet nose into her good hand, circled, then flumped down. Charlie heard creaking on the stairs and along the hallway.

"Charlie?" A voice whispered. "Are you awake?"

"Yes," she replied quietly. A second later Rosie, Alice and Mia pushed the door open, carrying plates laden with slices of pizza and salad into the room. They climbed onto the bed, sitting with their legs crossed under them.

"How's Phantom?" Charlie asked, taking the slice Rosie pushed towards her, and suddenly realising how hungry she was.

"Well, we've been checking him every five seconds," Rosie said. Charlie noticed Mia and Alice exchange worried looks.

"And?" Charlie persisted.

"Well, he's still not really settled," Mia told her hesitantly. "We'll check him again after we've finished this."

Charlie saw the worry in their faces, and climbed off the bed.

"Where are you off to?" Alice asked as Charlie

struggled to pull on another jumper. "We're meant to be making sure you don't wander off anywhere."

"If the look on your faces is anything to go by," Charlie said in a small voice, "I need to be on the yard with Phantom, not stuck up here. Especially if this is going to be my last night with him."

"Well, if you're going, we're coming with you," Alice replied. "Come on."

"Hang on a sec," Rosie protested. "What about this pizza? We can't just abandon it – it'll go cold!"

As the others followed Charlie, Rosie resignedly shoved half a slice of pizza in her mouth, much to Mia's disapproval. Rosie ignored her as they crept out of the room, down the stairs and past the living-room door which was pulled shut, muffled sounds of Christmas carols from the television and conversation coming from behind it.

Charlie pulled on her wellies and Alice helped her get her jacket on. She shivered as Mia opened the back door and the icy air swirled in. The Pony Detectives stepped into the dark and scrunched across the snow to the gate. Suddenly Rosie raised her hand and pointed as they looked across the yard.

"Pirate's stable door," she whispered, feeling a tingle race up her spine. "It's open!"

They looked at each other with thumping hearts. In the mayhem over Neve and Phantom, they'd forgotten all about the mystery of Pirate's escape!

Rosie and Alice grabbed each other's arms, as they quickly tiptoed across the dark yard towards Pirate's open stable door, Charlie and Mia following closely behind. There was no way they could check for footprints this time – the yard was covered in them. As they got closer they could just make out Pirate's shining eye from under his huge forelock – he was still inside.

But when they heard a shuffling coming from his stable they realised with thudding hearts that he wasn't alone.

The next second someone stepped out of the stable dressed all in black, a hoodie pulled down over their face. Both Rosie and Alice squealed while Mia lost her cool for a second and shrieked, terrified. Charlie thought she was going to faint again. But then the hooded figure shrank back against the stable door, looking as petrified as the Pony Detectives. As the stranger pulled their hood back, long black hair tumbled over their shoulders, and a pale face glowed in the moonlight.

"Neve!" Charlie cried. "What are you doing here? What are you doing in Pirate's stable?!"

"It's Phantom," Neve said urgently, her eyes filled with tears. "He's taken a turn for the worse, he looks seriously ill. I... I think it's colic, which if it isn't caught in time can be..."

"Fatal," Charlie said, her mouth dry as she

rushed to look over Phantom's door. Hettie was standing anxiously in the corner. Phantom was sweated up again and was pacing, his ears back as he turned his head to nip his sides, kicking at his belly with his hind hooves.

Neve looked directly at Charlie, her eyes filled with panic. "It... it's what Fable died of," she whispered. Charlie nodded, understanding. "This is all my fault! Just like before..."

"What do you mean?" Alice asked, but Neve ignored the question and carried on.

"I tried to ring granddad," she explained quickly, focusing again. "He... he'd know what to do – but his mobile's going straight to voice-mail and the landline's engaged. I thought the quickest thing to do would be to ride over there – I could cut across the footpath to the village. I was going to borrow one of your ponies to ride over; I didn't think you'd mind..."

"No, of course not," Charlie said quickly, suddenly feeling faint again. Neve nodded and dumped the rucksack she had slung over her shoulder. It fell sideways as she disappeared back into Pirate's stable; she vaulted onto his back, then ducked under the stable door lintel and rode him out into the yard, bareback on top of one of his rugs, with just his headcollar and lead rope to steer. Charlie's eyes widened at the sight. Then she noticed how bright Pirate looked, his ears pricked, excited by his moonlit adventure. Rosie had already rushed over to open the gate and without another word Neve trotted Pirate out of the yard, sitting easily as she urged him into canter up the drive.

Charlie's mind whirred as she let herself into Phantom's stable, slipping his headcollar over his hot, damp ears.

"She rode him straight from the stable," Mia said, coming to stand by the stable door.

"She must have walked around the edge of the yard, under the eaves where there wasn't any snow, then got on Pirate in his stable. That might explain why there weren't any footprints on the yard the other night," Alice said, thinking like a Pony Detective.

"And why Pirate's lead rope was clipped to the side of his headcollar again," Charlie added. "So it was ready for Neve to ride him."

"I saw Beanie playing around her earlier when she left the house," Mia remembered. "He was behaving like he knew her really well."

"But if she hadn't ever been to the yard, how would he know her?" Rosie said.

"Unless she'd been sneaking in when we weren't here," Mia said.

"But what I don't get is that she knew Charlie was looking for a new rider for Pirate," Alice frowned. "Why didn't she just ask?"

"I don't know," Charlie sighed, "but it's obvious how perfectly matched they are."

Mia ducked down to set the rucksack back upright. It was heavy and she noticed that it was stuffed with clothes. Then she saw something red that had fallen out of it and into the snow: Fable's diary.

"That's why I couldn't find it earlier!" Charlie said as Mia showed her.

"Neve got changed in Rosie's room," Mia said, "remember? She must have taken it then. And if she knew it was there, she must have been the one to drop it off for you."

"Looks like she was planning to run away again," Alice said. "Do you reckon she was going to take Pirate with her?"

Charlie shook her head. "I heard someone on the stairs earlier when my mum got here," she explained. "It was before you all came up, just before Neve left. If it was Neve she must have heard Mum saying that Phantom had to go. Phantom's her last connection to Fable and to her mum. She probably couldn't face the thought of losing him too. I bet she gave me the diary to try and help me keep him. But when that didn't work, I reckon she came back here to run away with him tonight."

"Only when she got back here she found he was ill," Rosie said, "so she changed her plans."

At that moment Phantom groaned, twisting his head round to bite violently at his side. Charlie's heart raced. She checked her watch. It felt like hours since Neve had disappeared into the night, but it had only been fifteen minutes. She stroked Phantom's neck, but he shook his head, then stretched it out, his hooves splayed in pain.

"What do you think Neve meant by everything being her fault?" Alice asked as she looked over to the drive, willing Neve to reappear as Mia went to put the diary back into the bag. As she did, a couple of loose pages tucked in the back, and a horse passport, fluttered to the floor.

Mia unfolded them, and started to read. "I think these might be the missing pages Charlie asked Fran Hope about," she whispered. Charlie looked up as Mia moved to the door, under the stable light. Mia scanned through them. "Caitlin writes about Neve being over the moon that Fable finally accepted an apple from her hand – only when she found Neve trying to give Fable another one, she had to tell her that she couldn't give Fable too many. That night Fable got colic – that's the last entry – with Caitlin waiting for her dad, Mr McCuthers, to arrive."

Charlie's breath caught in her throat. She couldn't let herself think about what happened to Fable – she had to concentrate on the here and now, not the past.

"And there's a passport here," Mia said, looking through it. She looked up slowly. "Guess what Fable's full name is?"

The others stared at her.

"Faraway Fable," she whispered. Any last possible bit of doubt over Phantom being Fable's foal vanished in an instant.

At that second they heard a jeep rumbling down the drive, crackling over frozen puddles, followed by headlight beams sweeping into the yard before the engine cut out. Charlie felt flooded with relief as car doors slammed and footsteps hurried through the gate. She came to the front of the stable and saw Mr McCuthers, carrying a large brown leather case. Alice looked beyond him, but there was no sign of Neve. They quickly exchanged hellos, but Mr McCuthers didn't waste a second.

"Right, let's see the patient," he said efficiently as Mia showed him which stable Phantom was in. He let himself straight into Phantom's stable. Charlie noticed, as she anxiously held the lead rope, that Mr McCuthers faltered for a moment, his eyes drinking in the black horse as he rested one hand on his hot neck.

"Now then, boy," he said under his breath, "I'm on your side, and it's time for you to fight."

As Hettie hid by Phantom's legs, Mr McCuthers eased back the black horse's rugs gently. He started to examine him expertly, checking his eyes, his gums, holding a stethoscope to his chest and to his abdomen in various places. Charlie stepped outside as Mr McCuthers began his treatment, giving Phantom an injection to ease the pain to start with then dipping in and out of his bag. After fifteen minutes he stepped out of the stable.

"This is a nasty case," he said in a quiet, soft voice. "I'll need to stay and monitor him for a bit, but be prepared – if he doesn't improve, we may need to take him for an operation. I'll call one of my colleagues and have them on standby, just in case."

They stood gathered anxiously by Phantom's door, and Rosie ran to the cottage to tell her parents what was happening. As Rosie's parents brought out cups of tea to warm everyone up, Mr McCuthers made his call. He kept checking Phantom while they waited for Neve to bring Pirate back.

"If she comes back at all," Rosie muttered. Mr McCuthers looked up sharply and Alice dug her in the ribs. Mia sighed and handed Mr McCuthers Neve's bag. He looked inside, his face dropping as he saw the clothes and realised what Rosie had meant. But at that moment they heard soft hoofbeats in the snow and turned to see Neve trotting back into the chilly stable-lit yard and sliding off Pirate. She popped him into the box next door, then rushed out to where the others were standing by Phantom's box.

"How's he doing?" Neve asked. Her hood was pulled up around her face, her long hair falling over one shoulder.

"He's hanging in there," Charlie said, "but he's not out of the woods yet."

Charlie heard a sniff and turned to see Neve's pale, tearstained face.

"I'm... I'm so sorry," Neve whispered, burying her face in her hands.

"It's okay, Neve," Charlie said quickly as Mr McCuthers stepped closer. "It's not your fault."

"It is!" Neve said hoarsely, fiddling with the string pull on her hoodie. "It's *all* my fault, all of it! You don't understand..."

"Hang on." Mia glanced at the others, then back at Neve. "You think Fable got colic and died because you gave her an apple, right?" she asked gently. Neve looked up sharply, her face distraught.

"Charlie read the diary but she noticed that some pages had been torn out," Alice explained.

"We found them tonight, when your bag tipped over and the diary fell out into the snow," Rosie added. "Is that why you tore them out, because your mum had written about you giving Fable an apple?"

Neve's cheeks flushed red for a second.

"It wasn't just one, that was the problem. I... I gave Fable two more, when Mum wasn't looking," Neve said hesitantly, with a shiver. "She never knew and I never told her afterwards, I was too scared. But I'd been so happy about Fable eating from my hand. Hours later she was dead." Neve gulped. "And if Fable hadn't died, Mum wouldn't have packed us up and gone to Ireland,

and if she hadn't gone to Ireland, maybe she might not have been..."

Neve sobbed, unable to continue.

"Neve, you were only five," Mr McCuthers cut in. "She didn't blame you at all for what happened. Fable's colic wasn't your fault. I tried my hardest, we all did, but Fable was just too weak to fight – that was the problem."

Neve looked unsure, her eyes puffy. "R-really? Mum didn't blame me? You're sure?"

"One hundred per cent," Mr McCuthers sighed.

"But... I thought..." Neve started, looking confused.

"Well you thought wrong," Mr McCuthers said firmly.

"But why did that make you want to run away?" Rosie asked as Neve stood, looking shocked.

"I... I didn't want to go back to Hope Farm," Neve said in barely a whisper. "I worried that Fran might have seen me feeding the extra apples to Fable. I couldn't face her..."

"But Fran can't wait for you to come back!" Mr McCuthers told her. "She was delighted when I told her we were looking for somewhere smaller to move to – she suggested the annexe and we thought it was perfect. She's over the moon about you staying – she hasn't stopped talking about it. She said you were just like your mum around horses and she can't wait for you to help her with the problem ponies – with all her plans for you, you're about to become very busy helping out at Hope Farm, in between school and homework that is!"

Suddenly it was like a huge weight had lifted off Neve's shoulders. She started to laugh with relief, only it turned into tears and her granddad gave her a warm hug.

"Come on," he said softly. "It's time we took you home."

Mr McCuthers popped back inside Phantom's

box to do one last check and pack up his bag.

"I've done as much as I can for now," he said to Charlie, resting one hand on Phantom's withers. "But you'll have to carry on making regular checks for the rest of the night. He could deteriorate and, if he does, I want you to ring this number and get Mr Honeycott to drive him straight to the vet's surgery. Ring me on the way and I'll meet you there. Okay?"

Charlie nodded as she took the number Mr McCuthers had scribbled down. "Thanks so much, for everything."

"I hope he's okay," Neve sniffed, taking one long last look over the stable door.

Mr McCuthers promised to come back first thing, then he and Neve headed across the yard. From the next stable Pirate looked out to watch them go. As Neve walked away to a new life filled with rescue ponies, Charlie wondered whether Pirate's chances of finding his perfect partner had just been shattered.

U U U U

"Is he going to be all right?" Rosie asked, peering over Phantom's stable door after the jeep had rumbled away.

"I don't know," Charlie replied honestly as she stroked Phantom's face. He didn't wrinkle his nose, or swish his tail. He just stood there, exhausted. There was a loud echoing, grumbling noise, then all of a sudden Phantom lifted his tail and broke wind violently, swiftly followed by a rapid-fire torrent of splattery droppings and a long, loud groan.

"Crikey!" Rosie squeaked, taking cover.

Suddenly Phantom's knees began to buckle. Rosie squealed as Charlie and Hettie side-stepped and Phantom went down on his front end then lowered his back end. He lay for a moment with his head up. Charlie stroked his forelock, pushing it to one side, then, tentatively knelt down next to him. Phantom didn't even blink.

"Look, he actually seems quite sweet," Alice whispered.

"He seems quite ill, more like," Rosie replied before Mia nudged her hard.

Charlie sat, stroking his neck. Suddenly he let out a long, juddering groan and laid his head down in Charlie's lap. He blinked a few times, as Charlie rested her hand on his cheek, bending her head down over his. She kissed his forehead, brushing her fallen tear from it. For a moment, everything in the yard was silent. Charlie hugged his neck gently, staying as quiet as she could.

"Er, is he dead?" Rosie whispered to Alice.

Charlie raised her head, her shoulders shaking and her eyes blurred.

"No, you idiot," she giggled through tears, "he's asleep!"

"Talking of which..." Rosie said, stifling another yawn.

"You three go back to bed," Charlie whispered, gently pulling Pirate's black, silky ear, as Hettie settled into a corner of the stable. "I'm not leaving Phantom tonight."

They nodded, but on the way back to the cottage Mia suggested that they should take it in turns through what was left of the night to check on both the patients at regular intervals.

"Ooh, bagsy I do my check at eight o'clock tomorrow morning," Rosie said, suddenly skidding on a patch of compacted snow by the gate. She lost her balance and landed flat on her back, sliding half under the gate and getting wedged. Mia had to help Alice pull her out, and all three were weak from giggling by the time they headed back inside.

As their laughter died away, Charlie looked down at the beautiful black horse. Her heart jolted as she thought of his stable at Blackberry Farm being empty; she suddenly couldn't imagine him not being there. Hearing his rhythmical, regular breathing, she started to feel tired.

"If you pull through," she whispered into his

mane, "I'll write *your* diary from now on, and I'll do everything I can to make all of the chapters the happiest they can be, I promise. But please, please, don't let tonight be your first chapter *and* your last."

She leaned back against the big bank of straw in the stable and closed her eyes, Phantom's warmth in her lap shutting out the bitter coldness beyond the stable walls.

Chapter Sixteen

CHARLIE rolled over sleepily.

"Phantom!" she whispered under her breath, almost falling out of bed. Charlie vaguely remembering being led half asleep up the stairs by Mrs Honeycott, just as dawn was breaking. She checked her watch – it was nearly ten! Then she realised what had woken her. She rushed to the window to see a large, shiny horsebox bump down the drive and pull up outside the yard. It was Mrs Millar! She watched as the trainer, dressed in smart jods, riding boots and a puffa jacket, walked to the back door. Charlie listened, her heart racing, as Mrs Millar was shown into the living room. She just heard Mrs Honeycott say that Charlie's parents were on their way as she quickly pulled her jumper on one-handed over the clothes she was still wearing from the night before. She hopped down the stairs two at a time, grabbed her wellies and raced out of the back door.

As she skidded up to the gate an unearthly, ghostly neigh echoed round the yard and stopped her in her tracks, taking her breath away. She looked up; there, with his striking head over the stable door for the first time ever, his ears pricked as he watched her, stood Phantom.

Charlie gulped, and held her breath in disbelief, wondering if she was dreaming.

She stood at the gate and blinked. But he was still there, his head upright, looking straight at her. The neigh echoed round again. Charlie's heart pounded, her hand shaking as she clambered clumsily over the gate and ran to his stable. He didn't flinch or rush out of sight; instead he reached his muzzle forward to greet her. Charlie stepped up and flung her good arm around his neck. Her eyes blurred as she buried her head in his mane.

"Now that", Rosie smiled as she let herself out of Dancer's stable, carrying her grooming kit, "was one powerful Christmas cake wish!"

Alice skipped over from the tack room as Mia pulled out her phone to take a picture. "Evidence," she explained, "just in case this is a one-off!"

As Charlie let herself into the stable, Hettie stepped forwards and Phantom suddenly pricked his ears.

Charlie heard a car pull up, then car doors slam. She looked round and saw Neve plumping through the snow in her wellies up to the gate, accompanied by her grandparents. Mr McCuthers walked into the yard and stepped over to Phantom's box to check on him. Charlie waited nervously for the vet's verdict. Phantom snorted gently and rubbed his head against Charlie's good arm.

"He's recovering well," Mr McCuthers

announced, breaking into a broad grin. Charlie beamed. As Mr McCuthers went to join Mrs McCuthers inside for a cup of tea, Neve stepped up to Phantom's door and stroked his neck.

"When did you work out that Phantom was Fable's foal?" Charlie asked, as the others gathered outside.

"Pretty much the first time I saw him," Neve smiled, shyly. "He's the spitting image of Fable, although I couldn't be sure. And when I saw that you were struggling with him, I thought of Mum's diary, so I sneaked into Hope Farm to get it. It felt horrible going in when Fran was out in one of the fields, but I wanted it so desperately, in case it could help Phantom. I should have just asked her for it, but I couldn't bring myself to talk to her – I was worried she blamed me for Fable's death. And I thought I'd lost the photo you'd found, too, so I took some of Fran's while I was there, and Fable's passport, as a keepsake."

"So that's why the Sellotape in the notebook

Fran showed us was still pretty sticky," Mia said, nodding.

"And I kept letting Hettie out, too," Neve said. "Molly helped Fable so much, I was sure Hettie would be just as good for Phantom."

Charlie smiled. Neve had been right. She let herself out of Phantom's stable and noticed Pirate looking out over his door. For a second her heart twinged, feeling terrible that his wish hadn't come true. Then Neve walked across to Pirate. His nostrils fluttered in a soft greeting as she found him a mint.

"I guess you'll have your hands full now," Charlie said quietly, "once you move into Hope Farm."

Neve nodded. "Although we popped into Fran's on the way over," she said, "and a lot of the rescue ponies can't be ridden, which means I'll be doing quite a bit of groundwork with them." Neve looked down and pulled something out of her pocket. "So, I was wondering if you were still looking for someone to take Pirate on loan..?"

"The adverts!" Charlie cried, seeing the crumpled postcards in Neve's hand.

Neve blushed. "I know I shouldn't have done it," she giggled, shyly, "but I came back here to see Phantom, to check if it really was him. Then I bumped into Pirate here, who was looking as down in the dumps and lonely as I was feeling. So I started to pop in and see him each day, giving him a bit of a groom. I hated not being around ponies and he was so sweet and cheeky, I... I kind of fell in love with him. And I couldn't resist having a quick ride, sorry Charlie."

"But why didn't you just ask about riding him in the first place, rather than creeping about the yard?" Rosie asked.

Neve's face clouded over again for a moment. "I didn't want to stay here," she explained quietly. "I wanted to be back in Ireland, but I wanted everything to be how it was before. Only I realised last night, even if I did go back, things could never be how they were ever again. Not without Mum."

Neve sighed as the girls exchanged glances, feeling terrible for her.

"Anyway, I didn't want to ask about riding Pirate as if nothing had happened," she continued, "because I worried that Nan and Granddad would think everything was okay and that I wanted to stay. But at the same time, I couldn't face losing Pirate after I'd just got to know him, not on top of losing everything else, so I took down the ads. And now that I *am* staying, I know that loaning Pirate will be the best way to help me settle in. He already feels like a best friend and he's so much fun!"

Charlie laughed. She was over the moon. She knew that Neve was the rider Pirate would have picked, a thousand times over. "Pirate would *love* you to take him on, and so would I."

At that moment they heard a car arrive and Charlie's stomach flipped. She knew that it would be her parents. They walked into the yard moments later as Mrs Millar came out of the cottage door.

Charlie took a deep breath and walked over to meet them all.

"Mum," she started, already knowing what she wanted to say, "about Phantom, please can I keep him? Yesterday really, truly wasn't his fault."

Charlie's mum looked at her for a moment, then over to Phantom.

"I don't know, Charlie," she said, watching her closely. "A week ago you didn't seem that bothered by the idea of losing him. What's changed all of a sudden?"

"We didn't trust each other," Charlie said simply, feeling her heart race faster and faster, "but we do now, everything's changed – look!"

Charlie led them over to Phantom's stable. He stepped towards her with his ears pricked as she let herself in quietly. The black horse fluttered his nostrils and Charlie gently cuddled his muzzle, dropping a kiss on his velveteen nose.

Mrs Millar gasped. "He's never been like that with anyone before!" she said.

"Well, I guess we could give him one more chance," her dad said finally.

"No," Charlie said firmly, "not one more chance, a million chances. I want him to know that he'll be safe here for ever, no matter what. Please?"

"I'm more than happy to come over and give you some lessons. We can do lots of work with Phantom on the ground, even if the paddock's too hard to ride on," Mrs Millar barked in her forthright voice. "I know you had a wonderful connection before when you competed together. You just need to get your confidence back up and you'll be amazing together, I can tell."

"So...?" Charlie asked, looking at her parents and hopping up and down.

"So, I guess we'd better give it a go then," her dad said, starting to smile. "Phantom can stay!"

Charlie let herself out of Phantom's stable and hugged her mum and dad wildly, her heart feeling as if it was going to burst. Then her parents headed off towards the cottage with Mrs Millar.

Neve walked over, looking hopeful.

"One last thing," Neve asked, biting her lip. "I know it's a huge thing to ask, but is there any chance I could keep Pirate at Hope Farm, now we're moving there?"

Charlie thought for a second. Deep down she'd always dreaded finding someone to loan Pirate because she never really wanted him to leave Blackberry Farm – but she realised that, with Neve, suddenly it felt right. As much as she'd miss him like crazy, she also knew that Neve would look after him like nobody else. Neve could look out of her bedroom window to talk to him whenever she wanted, just as she'd read in the diary her mum, Caitlin, had once done with Fable. And Hope Farm wasn't far, so Charlie could visit loads – it was perfect, and Pirate would be in heaven there. She took a deep breath, then nodded.

Charlie helped Neve tack up, giving Pirate hundreds of mints and kisses, and Alice, Mia and Rosie piled his gear into Mr and Mrs McCuthers'

car. Charlie gave Pirate the biggest hug ever before Neve jumped into the saddle. With a wave, she rode off, grinning, and promising to ride back and visit loads and inviting them to ride over whenever they could.

As Neve and Pirate disappeared up the drive, Rosie suddenly scooted off towards the house, calling over her shoulder that it was time for a celebration. She came back a few moments later, with Beanie racing beside her, scattering the clucking chickens as they went, and carrying a plate laden with thick wedges of Christmas cake. Alice, Mia and Charlie all helped themselves to a piece.

"To the Pony Detectives," Mia toasted. "For successfully uncovering who was behind the mystery of Pirate's escape and the black hairs in my grooming kit!"

"Well, yes, eventually," Rosie grinned, taking a huge mouthful of her own piece of cake.

"And for working out where Neve had gone,"

Alice added, "*and* why she wanted to run away."

"That's five cases we've solved now." Charlie smiled, biting into her slice. "Who knows what the next one will—" But she stopped suddenly, as her teeth clonked on something hard.

"Ow!" she mumbled, fishing around until she pulled something out of her mouth. "What's that?"

"It's the coin!" Rosie cried as they all crowded round. "You get another wish!"

Charlie looked around at her three best friends, standing in the snow in the ramshackle yard, with four happy ponies looking over their stable doors. Pirate might have left Blackberry Farm, but he was heading off to start a whole new adventure with the perfect partner to look after him.

"I don't need another wish," Charlie beamed, slipping the coin into her pocket. "I've already got everything I could possibly wish for, right here."

Mia's Guide to Cleaning Your Bridle

Cleaning tack isn't always a popular task at the yard, but it's one of the most important!

Why is it so important?

ᕟ It keeps the tack supple, so it won't rub your pony or crack and break when you're riding (which is dangerous).

ᕟ It makes your pony look lovely and smart!

TOP TIP!
Remember to wash your bit after every ride. A dirty bit is not nice for your pony to put in his mouth!

How to clean your bridle:

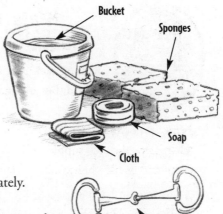

1 Strip your bridle down – this means taking it completely apart. Undo all the buckles and lay out all the leather straps separately.

2 Wash the bit and leave it to dry.

3 Grab a sponge, dip it in warm water and clean the grime off all the straps and buckles. Be careful not to soak the leather.

4 Once the bridle is dry, take another sponge and make it slightly damp. Rub some saddle soap on the sponge, then rub it on the leather.

5 Buff the leather with a clean, dry cloth to make it shine!

6 Put the bridle back together again and reattach the bit.

TOP TIP!
Remember which hole each strap was done up on before you take it apart. That way, it'll be exactly the same size when you put it back together!

Mr McCuthers' Guide to Colic

Colic is the horsey equivalent of tummy ache. You should always call a vet if you think your pony might have colic.

Signs to look out for:

◡ Pawing at the ground

◡ Turning his head to look at his tummy. He might start nipping or kicking at his tummy too.

◡ Restlessness and getting down to roll

◡ Lying down more than usual

◡ Lots of gut noise, or none at all. There should always be a little noise in your pony's tummy – you can hear it if you put your ear to his side when he's well.

◡ Sweating up

◡ Increased heart rate and breathing faster than normal, sometimes with flared nostrils

DID YOU KNOW?
Horses and ponies can't be sick. So when they get colic, the problem can only move in one direction...!

Some causes of colic:

- A change in routine, amount of exercise or diet
- A change of yard
- Stress

How to help your pony avoid getting it:

- Make sure his feed is good quality and that he always has access to clean water
- Worm your pony regularly
- Always ensure that any changes to his routine are introduced slowly

TOP TIP!
When you've called the vet, keep your pony warm and give him fresh water (but take any food away).

The Pony Detectives' Guide to Bareback Riding

Nothing makes you feel closer to your pony than riding him bareback. But it can be tricky, so before you try it, check out our top five tips!

1 For your first go at riding bareback, choose a really steady pony and <u>always</u> wear your hat!

DON'T FORGET
Ponies' coats are glossy if they're well groomed – it's very easy to slide around when you're up there!

2 Think about your position and try not to wriggle too much! Without a saddle between you, you'll feel all your pony's muscles moving and he'll feel every move you make too.

3 Remember that it's not just you who has to get used to riding without a saddle – your pony will take time to get used to it as well.

4 If you feel like you're getting a bit wobbly, grip onto your pony's mane to help you stay on. Don't use the reins to balance, you might hurt your pony's mouth.

5 And, most importantly… don't forget to have fun!